Childr
Rock
401 -
Rock Island, IL 61201-8143

W9-BUH-695

OCT 2010

School OF EVIL

Marie P. Croall

ILLUSTRATED BY Sandy Carruthers

GRAPHIC UNIVERSE™ · MINNEAPOLIS · NEW YORK

Story by Marie P. Croall

Pencils and inks by Sandy Carruthers

Coloring by Hi-Fi Design

Lettering by Marshall Dillon

Copyright © 2010 by Lerner Publishing Group, Inc.

Graphic Universe™ is a trademark and Twisted Journeys® is a registered trademark of
Lerner Publishing Group, Inc.

All rights reserved. International copyright secured. No part of this book may be reproduced,
stored in a retrieval system, or transmitted in any form or by any means—electronic, mechanical,
photocopying, recording, or otherwise—without the prior written permission of Lerner Publishing
Group, Inc., except for the inclusion of brief quotations in an acknowledged review.

Graphic Universe™
A division of Lerner Publishing Group, Inc.
241 First Avenue North
Minneapolis, MN 55401 U.S.A.

Website address: www.lernerbooks.com

Library of Congress Cataloging-in-Publication Data

Croall, Marie P.
  School of evil / by Marie P. Croall ; illustrated by Sandy Carruthers.
    p. cm. — (Twisted journeys)
  Summary: As the hero of this graphic novel who is attending a spooky boarding school, the
reader is asked to make choices throughout the story to avoid being harmed by strange, half-
human creatures.
  ISBN: 978-0-8225-9263-1 (lib. bdg. : alk. paper)
  1. Plot-your-own stories. 2. Graphic novels. [1. Graphic novels. 2. Boarding schools—Fiction.
3. Schools—Fiction. 4. Horror stories. 5. Plot-your-own stories.] I. Carruthers, Sandy, ill. II. Title.
PZ7.7.C76Sc 2010
741.5'973—dc22   2009013877

Manufactured in the United States of America
1 – DP – 12/15/2009

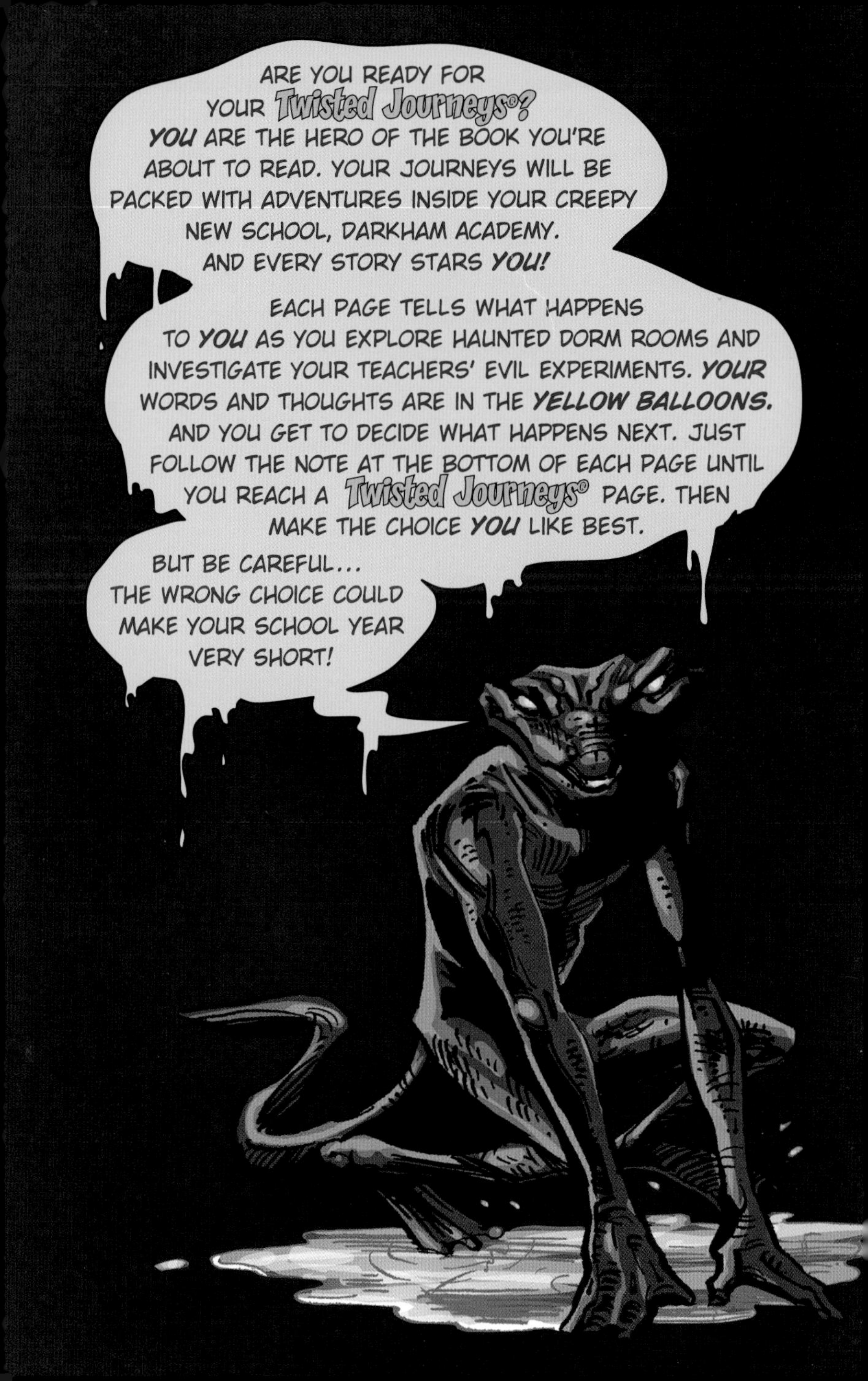
ARE YOU READY FOR YOUR Twisted Journeys®? YOU ARE THE HERO OF THE BOOK YOU'RE ABOUT TO READ. YOUR JOURNEYS WILL BE PACKED WITH ADVENTURES INSIDE YOUR CREEPY NEW SCHOOL, DARKHAM ACADEMY. AND EVERY STORY STARS YOU!
EACH PAGE TELLS WHAT HAPPENS TO YOU AS YOU EXPLORE HAUNTED DORM ROOMS AND INVESTIGATE YOUR TEACHERS' EVIL EXPERIMENTS. YOUR WORDS AND THOUGHTS ARE IN THE YELLOW BALLOONS. AND YOU GET TO DECIDE WHAT HAPPENS NEXT. JUST FOLLOW THE NOTE AT THE BOTTOM OF EACH PAGE UNTIL YOU REACH A Twisted Journeys® PAGE. THEN MAKE THE CHOICE YOU LIKE BEST.
BUT BE CAREFUL... THE WRONG CHOICE COULD MAKE YOUR SCHOOL YEAR VERY SHORT!

An old mansion looms over you, dark and spooky even in the morning light. For the next eight months, you will be living here at the Darkham Academy, an exclusive school for children of all ages. Looking at the place, you feel nervous for the first time. The building seems more like a haunted house than a school. In the distance, you can see what looks to be a river.

Your new classmates are gathering in the front yard, waiting for the first bell to ring. You walk through the gate of the iron fence that surrounds the school grounds and join them.

"Can you believe this is our school? Isn't it cool?" The girl standing next to you smiles happily at you. "I'm Jess. I'm here on a science scholarship, what about you?"

"I'm here for history." You smile back at Jess, feeling much better now that you know someone.

GO ON TO THE NEXT PAGE.

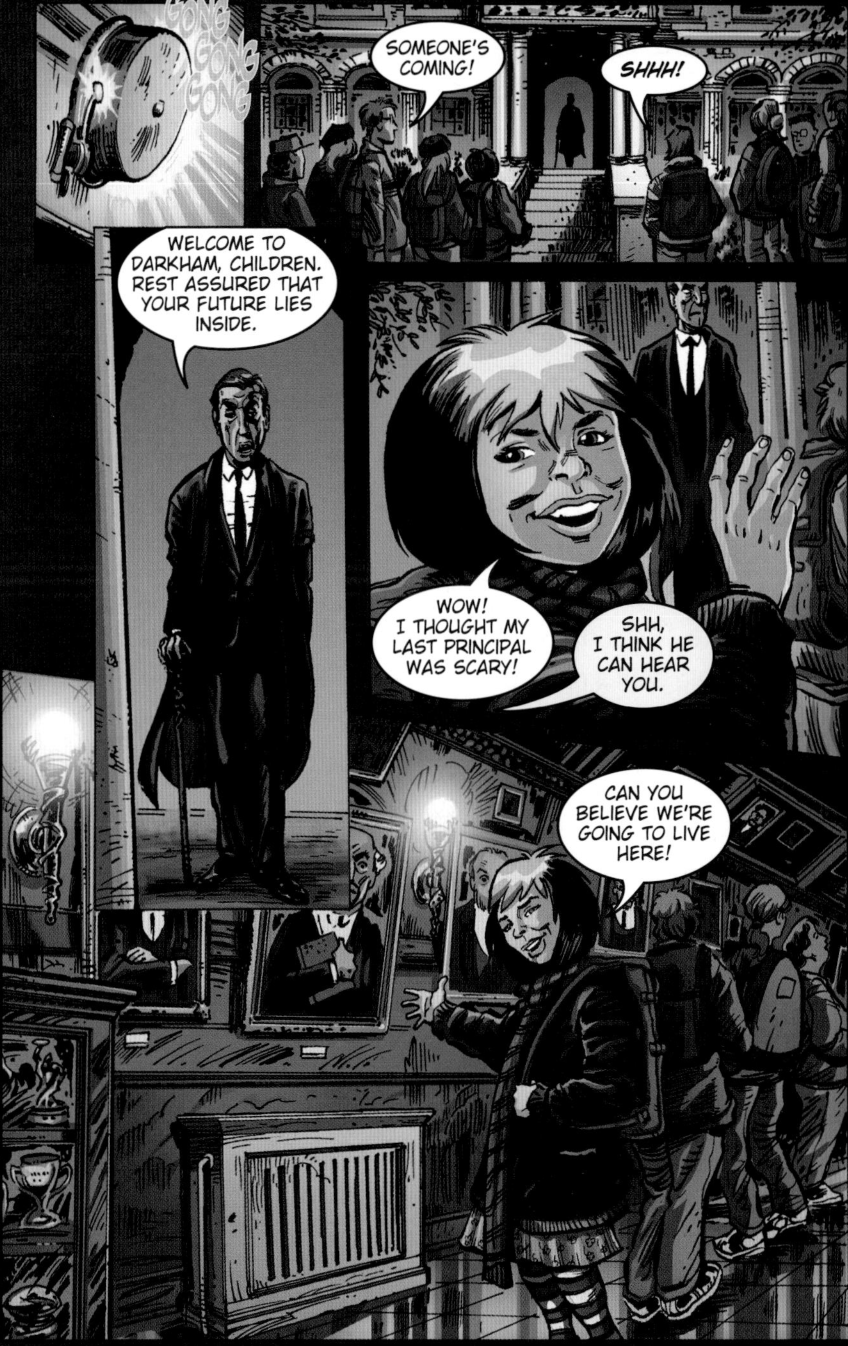
GONG GONG GONG
SOMEONE'S COMING!
SHHH!
WELCOME TO DARKHAM, CHILDREN. REST ASSURED THAT YOUR FUTURE LIES INSIDE.
WOW! I THOUGHT MY LAST PRINCIPAL WAS SCARY!
SHH, I THINK HE CAN HEAR YOU.
CAN YOU BELIEVE WE'RE GOING TO LIVE HERE!

GO ON TO THE NEXT PAGE.

You follow Jess into your first classroom. At the front of the room, a tall, thin woman with jet black hair pulled back into a tight bun stands behind a dark wooden podium. A thick book lies open on top of the stand.

"You are wasting valuable time, children," she says. "I am your history teacher, Professor Aslem. Take your seats, and we will begin the first lesson: Ancient Mythology."

You and Jess take the only seats left, way in the back of the classroom.

"Today we will be learning about—" A knock at the door interrupts the teacher. "Come in," she snaps.

A young man opens the door and pokes his head inside. "Headmaster Malone needs a couple of students to help with a project."

Jess whispers to you as she raises her hand. "I want to see what else goes on around here. What about you?"

GO ON TO THE NEXT PAGE.

You can go with Jess and the young man to help Headmaster Malone, or you can stay in Professor Aslem's class.

WILL YOU . . .

. . . go with Jess?
TURN TO PAGE 22.

. . . stay in the class?
TURN TO PAGE 46.

As you reach out your hand toward the red button, the thing in the tank stops banging on the lid. Although you can't see its face, you can feel it watching you. You take a deep breath and push the button.

Click.

You whirl around to look at the tank. A red light flickers on as the water begins to drain from the glass enclosure. The thing in the tank sinks to the bottom. You thought the "Open" button would just open the tank! You knock on the glass desperately, afraid that by draining the water you might have hurt the creature.

You crouch down and stare into the tank, watching the creature. You sigh in relief when you see its chest slowly moving up and down, breathing air.

Desperate to help the creature, you look around for something that will aid you. There's a ladder in the corner of the room, but not much else.

GO ON TO THE NEXT PAGE.

WILL YOU . . .

. . . use the ladder?
TURN TO PAGE 25.

. . . get help from a teacher?
TURN TO PAGE 86.

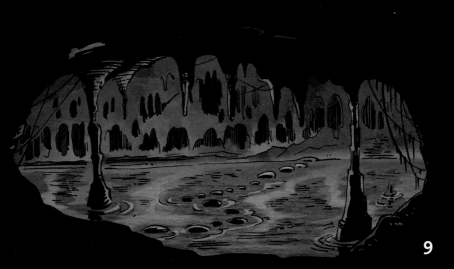

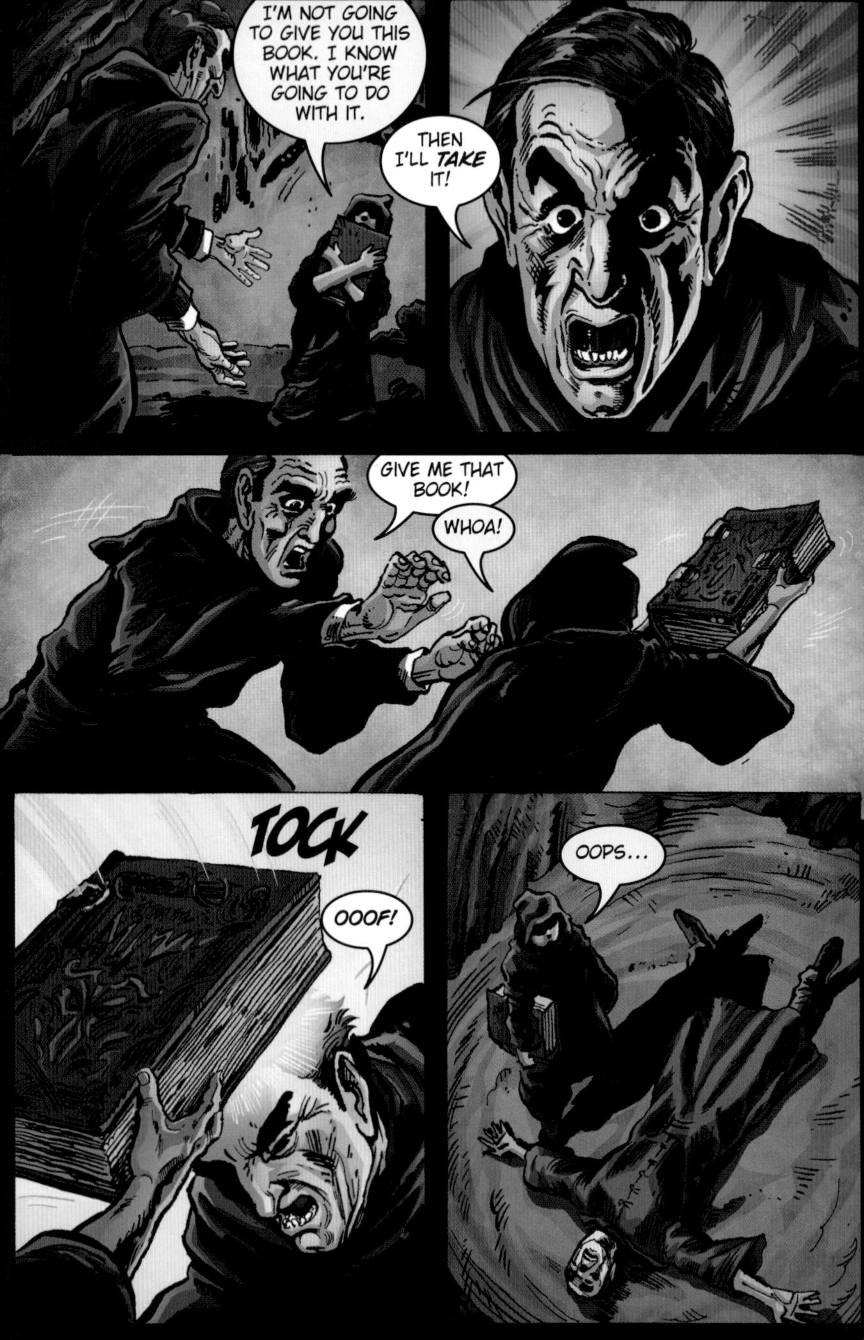
I'M NOT GOING TO GIVE YOU THIS BOOK. I KNOW WHAT YOU'RE GOING TO DO WITH IT.
THEN I'LL *TAKE* IT!
GIVE ME THAT BOOK!
WHOA!
TOCK
OOOF!
OOPS...

GO ON TO THE NEXT PAGE.

With the headmaster out cold, you take off in the direction Jess was heading. When you reach the big cavern with the pools of water, you can hear Jess taunting the other teachers again, and it sounds like they're running right toward you.

But wait—you're holding a book of magic, right? Hidden behind a rock, you quickly flip through the book, looking for some sort of spell to help you. When you find one that transforms stone to mud, you decide that's the quickest way to slow the teachers down.

You begin to recite the spell as Jessica runs past you. As you finish the incantation, you point at the ground under the teachers' feet. A bright light fills the cavern, and you start to get a sinking feeling . . . literally. Instead of just part of the floor, you've liquefied the entire cavern. And you're headed straight down!

Perhaps playing with magic wasn't the best idea after all . . .

THE END

Letting the creature out of the tank seems like a bad idea, since you don't really have any idea what kind of creature it is. You walk up to the glass to try to get a better look at the thing. Placing your hands on the glass, you lean close to the tank, peering in.

The creature in the tank swims up close to the glass, grimacing at you and revealing a row of pointy reptilian fangs. You jump away, horrified that the thing seems to be trying *on purpose* to scare you. You back away from the tank, suddenly wanting to be in your nice, safe, dry dorm room.

You make your way back to bed—determined never to go wandering around like this again. Yet you can't help but wonder which class involves studying the creatures in those labs.

Whatever it is, it's not a class you want to sign up for. Maybe you could take shop instead.

THE END

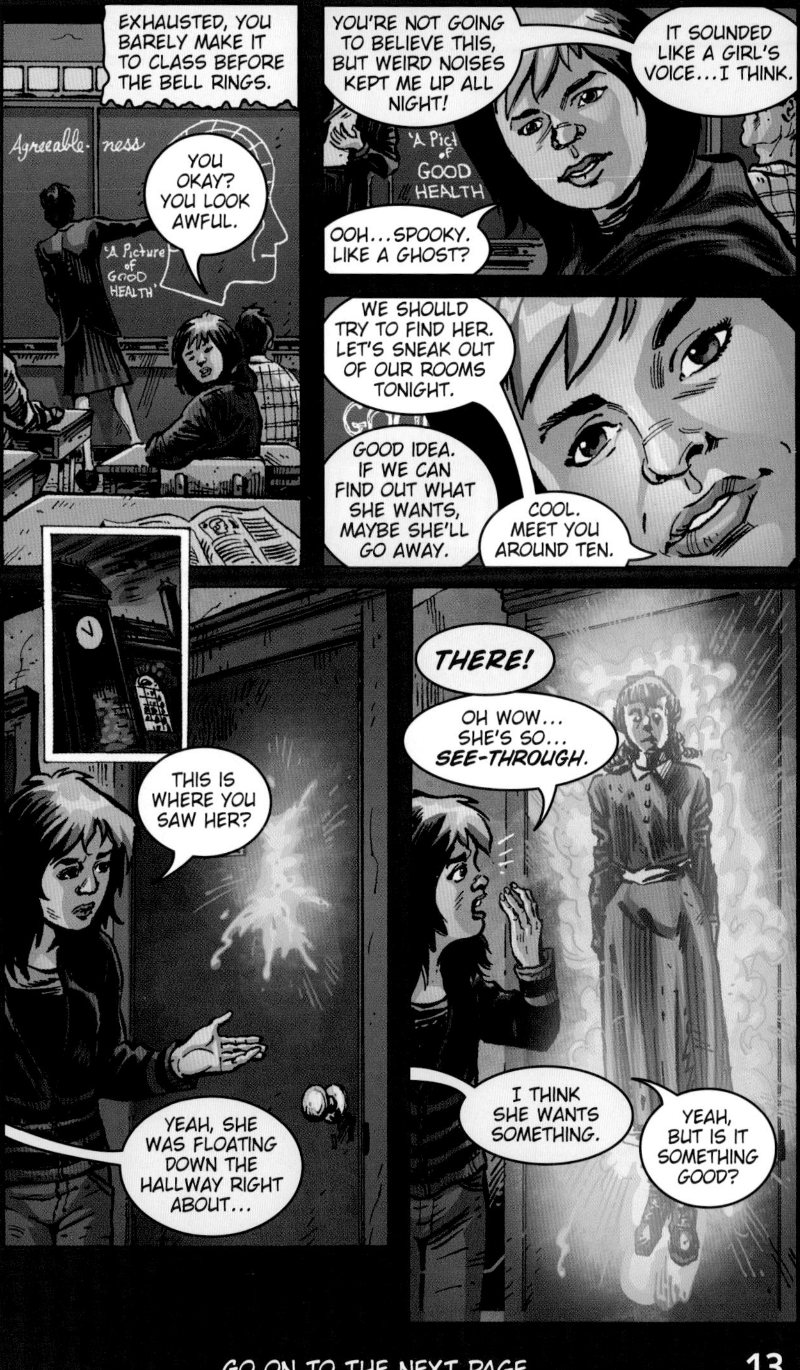
EXHAUSTED, YOU BARELY MAKE IT TO CLASS BEFORE THE BELL RINGS.
Agreeable-ness
'A Picture of Good Health'
YOU OKAY? YOU LOOK AWFUL.
YOU'RE NOT GOING TO BELIEVE THIS, BUT WEIRD NOISES KEPT ME UP ALL NIGHT!
IT SOUNDED LIKE A GIRL'S VOICE...I THINK.
OOH...SPOOKY. LIKE A GHOST?
WE SHOULD TRY TO FIND HER. LET'S SNEAK OUT OF OUR ROOMS TONIGHT.
GOOD IDEA. IF WE CAN FIND OUT WHAT SHE WANTS, MAYBE SHE'LL GO AWAY.
COOL. MEET YOU AROUND TEN.
THIS IS WHERE YOU SAW HER?
YEAH, SHE WAS FLOATING DOWN THE HALLWAY RIGHT ABOUT...
THERE!
OH WOW... SHE'S SO... SEE-THROUGH.
I THINK SHE WANTS SOMETHING.
YEAH, BUT IS IT SOMETHING GOOD?

GO ON TO THE NEXT PAGE.

As the spirit floats toward you, it looks as if she's trying to communicate with you.

WILL YOU . . .

. . . try to speak with her?
TURN TO PAGE 42.

. . . try to get away from her?
TURN TO PAGE 35.

"Run!" you shout at Jess, as you turn and sprint toward the path. As your feet hit the path, you see the monster slide into the water and begin swimming toward you. You look over your shoulder to check on Jess just in time to see her slip on the wet stones and tumble into the pool.

You immediately run back to her. Dropping to your knees, you reach out for her as she swims toward you, the monster close on her heels. You pull her out, but as the two of you start to run again, the water fills with the glowing eyes of dozens of creatures like the one chasing you.

You both freeze. Perhaps if you stay very still they won't see you . . .

. . . but then the monsters swarm onto the path.

THE END

You head toward the front door, hoping that the creature's first thought was to get out of the school. As you tiptoe toward the large door, you hear a scream and a loud crash from behind you. You whirl around in time to see the lizard creature race down the hall from the direction of the library. Hot on its heels is an angry teacher waving a broom.

The lizard heads up the stairs toward the lab. As it disappears into the darkness, the teacher stops right in front of you.

"I'm assuming you have a good reason for being out of bed and you know nothing about that thing?"

You squeak out a nervous, "I . . . um . . . got lost, ma'am." You scurry back to your dorm room, knowing that the teacher will take care of the lizard . . .

. . . and that in the morning, you're going to be in a *lot* of trouble.

16

THE END

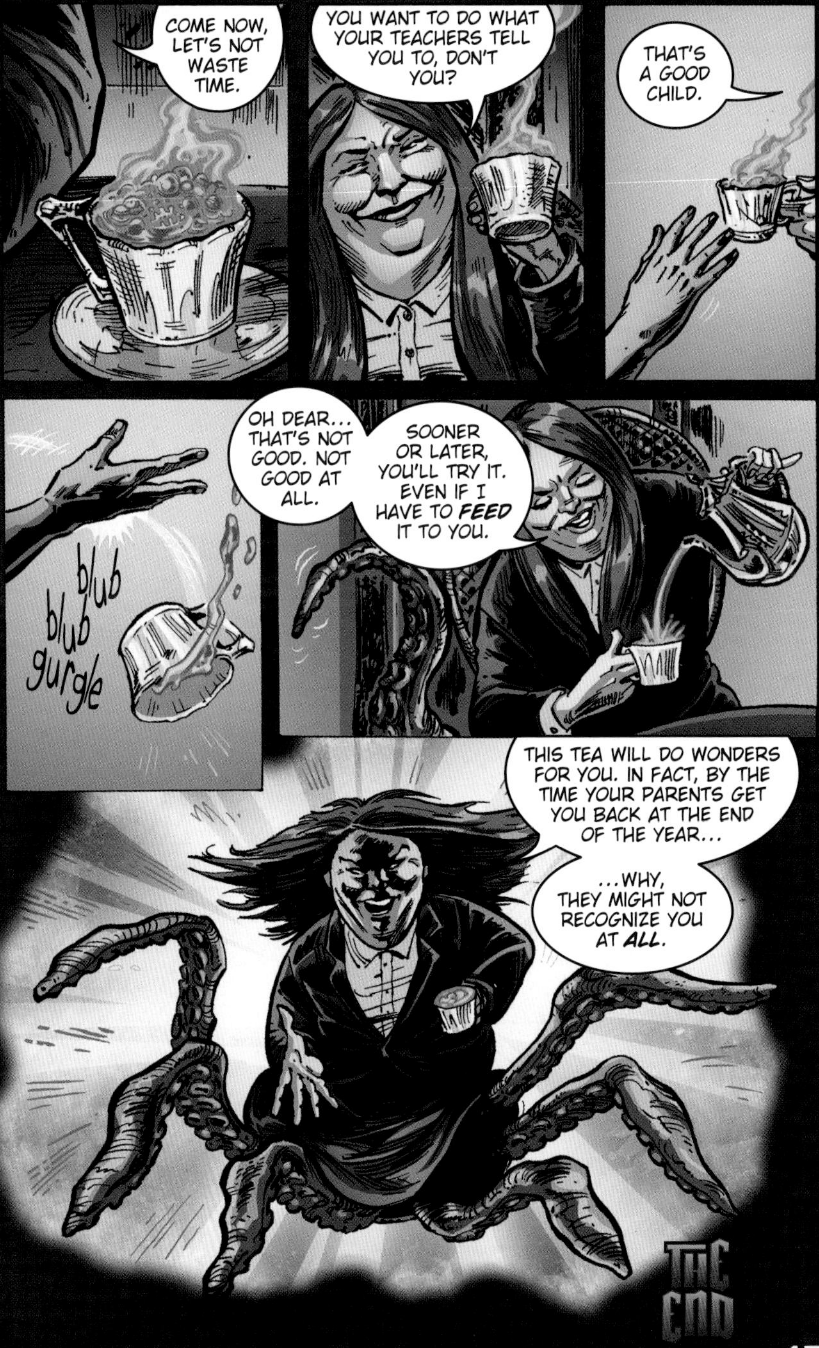
COME NOW, LET'S NOT WASTE TIME.
YOU WANT TO DO WHAT YOUR TEACHERS TELL YOU TO, DON'T YOU?
THAT'S A GOOD CHILD.
blub blub gurgle
OH DEAR... THAT'S NOT GOOD. NOT GOOD AT ALL.
SOONER OR LATER, YOU'LL TRY IT. EVEN IF I HAVE TO ***FEED*** IT TO YOU.
THIS TEA WILL DO WONDERS FOR YOU. IN FACT, BY THE TIME YOUR PARENTS GET YOU BACK AT THE END OF THE YEAR...
...WHY, THEY MIGHT NOT RECOGNIZE YOU AT ***ALL***.
THE END

You creep to the door of your room, moving quietly so whoever is in the hallway doesn't hear you coming. You press your ear up against the door, listening to make sure that the noises have passed by. Slowly you open the door and peer out.

You can see something moving down the hallway toward a part of the school you haven't visited yet. You sneak out the door and quickly follow.

Before too long, you come to the end of the hall and a large wooden door. Through the door, you hear the same groaning you heard in your room.

You pull the heavy door open to find a dark, steep staircase leading up to a floor you didn't know existed. With one hand on the wall for balance, you slowly climb the stairs.

GO ON TO THE NEXT PAGE.

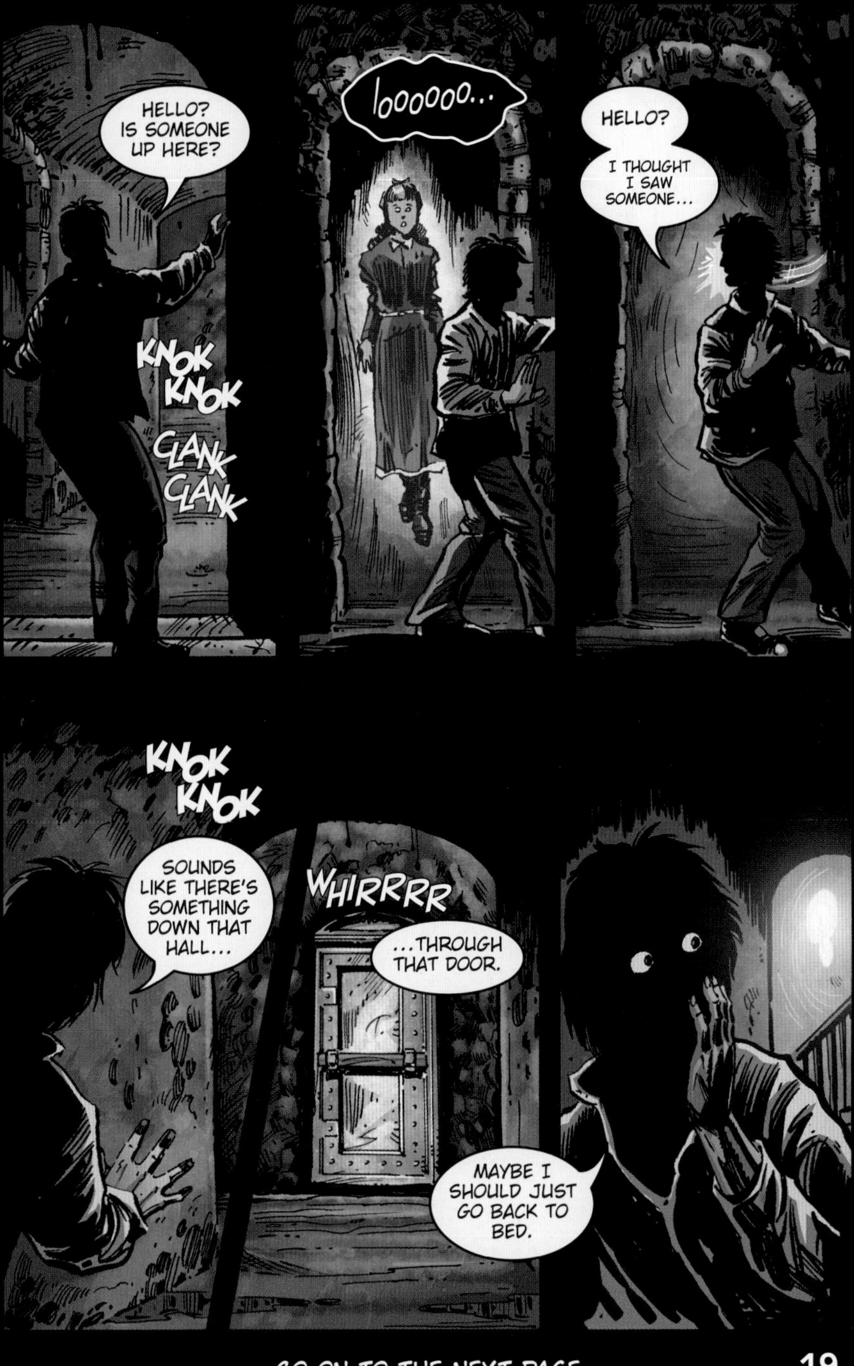
HELLO? IS SOMEONE UP HERE?
KNOK KNOK
CLANK CLANK
looooooo...
HELLO?
I THOUGHT I SAW SOMEONE...
KNOK KNOK
SOUNDS LIKE THERE'S SOMETHING DOWN THAT HALL...
WHIRRRR
...THROUGH THAT DOOR.
MAYBE I SHOULD JUST GO BACK TO BED.

GO ON TO THE NEXT PAGE.

You've just found a strange new part of the school to explore!

WILL YOU . . .

. . . go back to your room?
TURN TO PAGE 28.

. . . explore the hallway to your left?
TURN TO PAGE 40.

. . . go through the metal door ahead of you?
TURN TO PAGE 59.

"On the count of three," you whisper to Jess, "we're going to push the boulder onto the monster." Jess nods silently, biting her lip nervously. "You push from that side. I'll get this side."

Crouched behind the boulder, you sit and wait. The three seconds that it takes for the monster to reach you stretch out. You grab the boulder and nod at Jess. "One. Two. THREE!"

Together the two of you shove the rock with all your might. It resists slightly and then topples over directly on top of the monster, squishing it seconds before it would have reached you.

Exhausted, you and Jess sink to the ground. She looks over at you, smiling mischievously. "So . . . what do we tell Headmaster Malone when he asks where we were?"

"Biology lessons? Amphibians 101?" The two of you burst into gales of laughter, knowing that no amount of schoolwork will ever be as scary as your first day at Darkham.

THE END 21

You, Jess, and the young man walk to a staircase that spirals down into the basement. The young man stops at the top of the stairs, fidgeting nervously.

"Go to the headmaster's office at the end of the hallway, and *don't touch anything*," he says. You walk down the stairs as the young man heads back to his class.

The stairs open out onto a long, cold, stone hallway with dark wooden doors on each side. Between the doors, stone sconces in the shape of hands hold flickering lanterns.

"Do you think a lot of schools have basements like this?" you whisper nervously to Jess.

She shakes her head as you arrive at the office. Jess knocks on the door, and the two of you stand there waiting for what feels like an hour.

"I don't think anyone's in there," Jess whispers. "Let's go inside and wait."

GO ON TO THE NEXT PAGE.

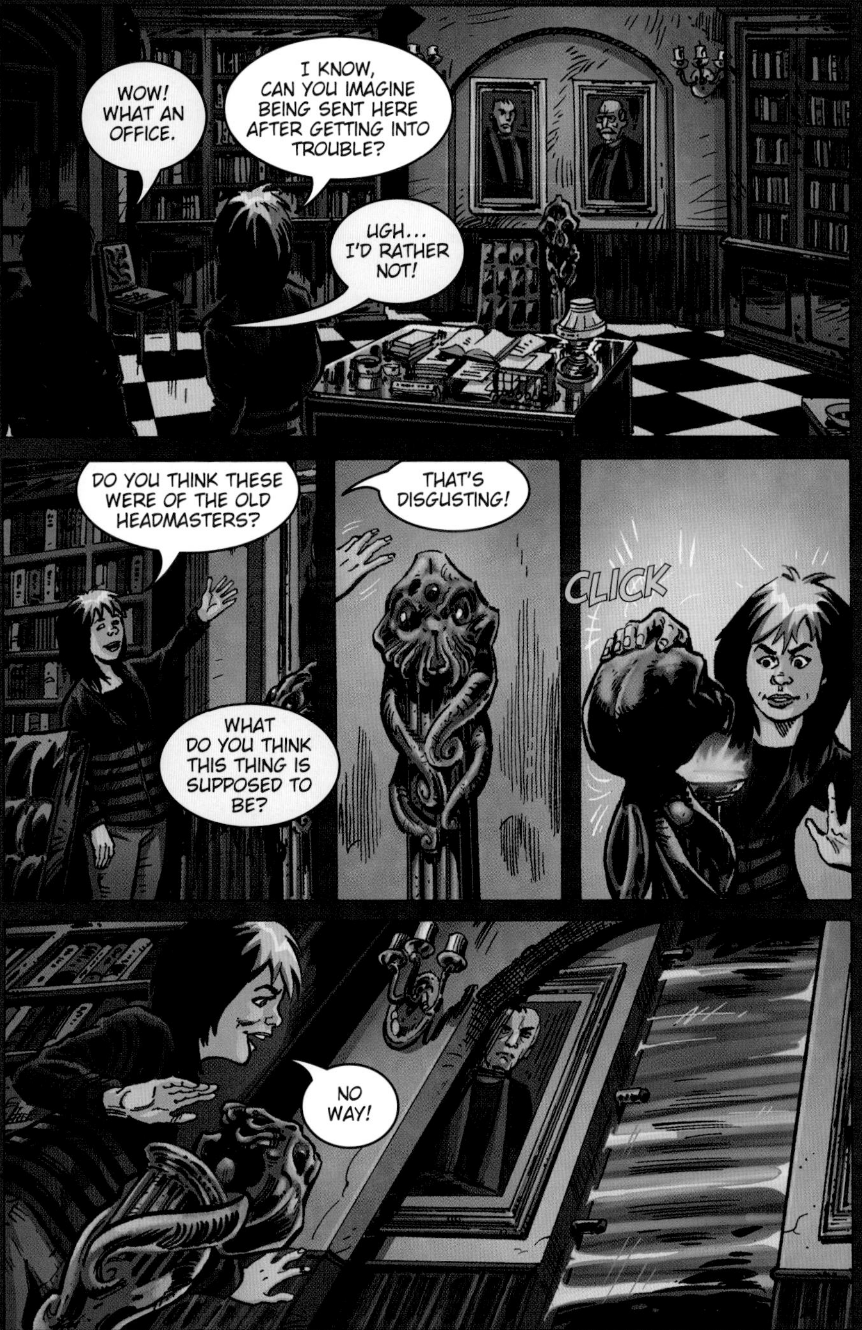
WOW! WHAT AN OFFICE.
I KNOW, CAN YOU IMAGINE BEING SENT HERE AFTER GETTING INTO TROUBLE?
UGH... I'D RATHER NOT!
DO YOU THINK THESE WERE OF THE OLD HEADMASTERS?
WHAT DO YOU THINK THIS THING IS SUPPOSED TO BE?
THAT'S DISGUSTING!
CLICK
NO WAY!

GO ON TO THE NEXT PAGE.

Jess has opened a secret passage!

WILL YOU . . .

. . . explore the passage?
TURN TO PAGE 43.

. . . stay and wait for the headmaster?
TURN TO PAGE 32.

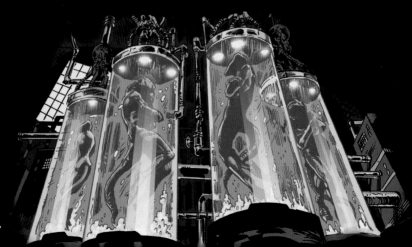

You drag the ladder to the side of the aquarium. As quickly as you can, you scramble up the rungs.

Peering into the tank, you can see a spigot at the bottom. You take a deep breath and leap into the empty tank to turn on the faucet. As you land, the creature looks up and growls at you.

You jump and stretch your arms up, but the top of the aquarium is too far for you to reach. The creature seems much healthier now that you're within claw range.

Although you can't be sure, it seems that the lizard creature is smiling at you as it starts to slither menacingly in your direction.

THE END

GET *BACK* HERE!

UGH... IT'S SO HEAVY.

OOOPS.

OH...THAT'S... NOT GOOD.

THUMP

CEPHALOAR

GO ON TO THE NEXT PAGE.

WILL YOU . . .

. . . dive into the water to escape whatever
magic you've unleashed?
TURN TO PAGE 53.

. . . throw the book into the water?
TURN TO PAGE 39.

. . . give the book back to Headmaster Malone?
TURN TO PAGE 102.

. . . read from the book?
TURN TO PAGE 78.

As you stand in the hallway listening to the strange noises, you decide that exploring strange parts of a new school is probably the fastest way to get expelled. You turn around and head back to your room. As you walk back down the stairs, you hear faint whispers. You turn to see if anyone is following you, but no one is there.

You make it back to your room, tuck yourself into bed, and try to go back to sleep. But every time you close your eyes, you hear the whispers again. You toss and turn all night, barely getting any sleep.

When the sun finally begins to rise, you groan, realizing that your first class starts in less than an hour. But you feel horrible. Maybe it would be better if you took a sick day and tried to get more sleep.

GO ON TO THE NEXT PAGE.

WILL YOU . . .

. . . try to make it through the day?

TURN TO PAGE 13.

. . . skip class?

TURN TO PAGE 57.

You head to the library, listening for the creature. At the heavy wooden door, you can hear muffled thumps coming from the other side.

Slowly you push the door open. The thumps get louder as you move through the bookshelves. Near the back wall, you see the lizard sitting behind a pile of books, gnawing on an encyclopedia.

It looks up at you curiously as it picks up a book and takes a bite out of it. An idea occurs to you, and you grab the top book of the stack, waving it at the lizard. It hops to its feet and greedily follows you back to the lab.

You toss the book into the lab. The lizard runs in after its snack, and you lock the door behind it.

That lizard wasn't so vicious after all. You promise yourself that you'll bring it a book once a week. Maybe you could tame it for a class project.

For extra credit, maybe you can even teach it to read the books instead of eating them.

THE END

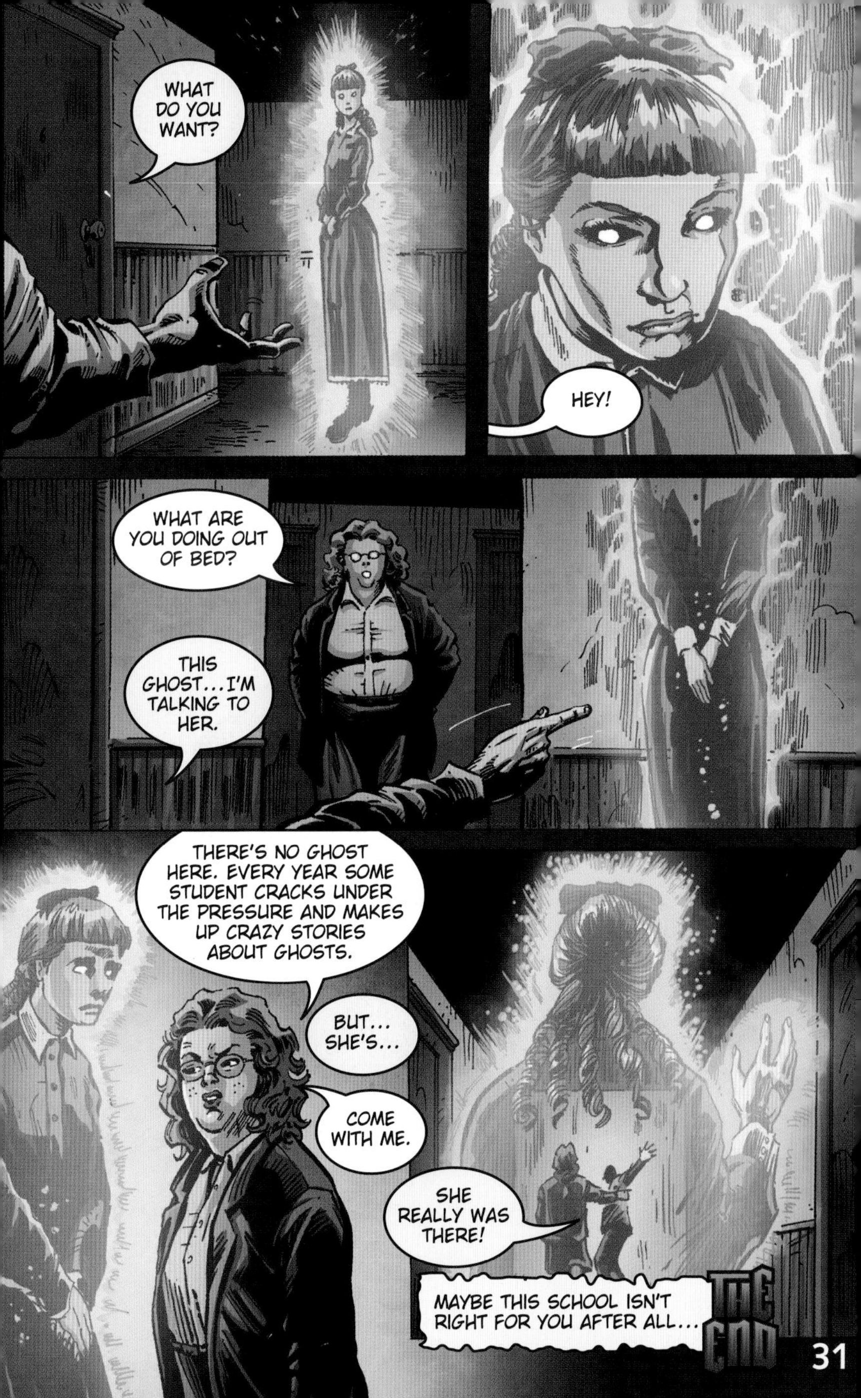
WHAT DO YOU WANT?
HEY!
WHAT ARE YOU DOING OUT OF BED?
THIS GHOST...I'M TALKING TO HER.
THERE'S NO GHOST HERE. EVERY YEAR SOME STUDENT CRACKS UNDER THE PRESSURE AND MAKES UP CRAZY STORIES ABOUT GHOSTS.
BUT... SHE'S...
COME WITH ME.
SHE REALLY WAS THERE!
MAYBE THIS SCHOOL ISN'T RIGHT FOR YOU AFTER ALL...
THE END

"Oh my gosh, someone's coming!" Jess squeals. You jump up and grab the edge of the door, pulling it closed as Jess struggles to set the statue back in place. You manage to put the room back the way it was just as the headmaster walks through the door. He raises an eyebrow at the two of you.

"I hope you weren't waiting long," he says slyly. "Several times each year, I ask for volunteers to help out with special projects. You two are the first of those volunteers this term. Jessica, if you will be so kind as to wait in the room across the hall, I have a *very* special job for our friend here."

Jess glances over her shoulder at you as she leaves the room. She looks scared as the door closes behind her. Waving for you to follow, the headmaster places a hand on the statue, opening the secret passage.

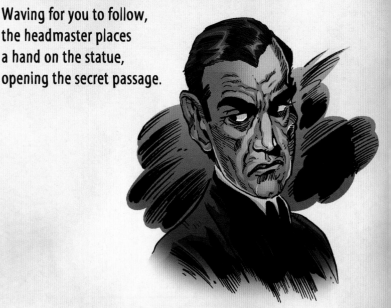

GO ON TO THE NEXT PAGE.

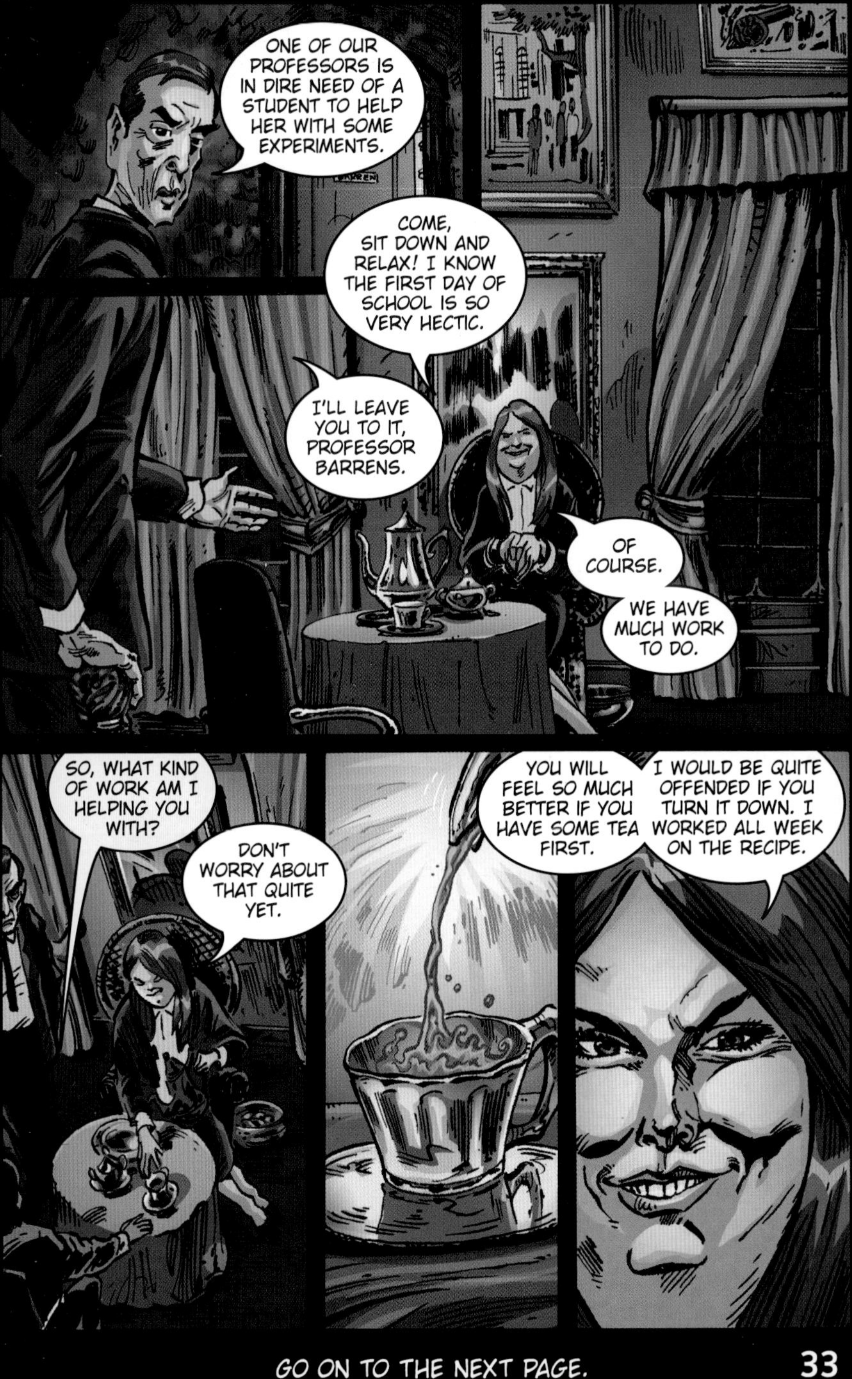
ONE OF OUR PROFESSORS IS IN DIRE NEED OF A STUDENT TO HELP HER WITH SOME EXPERIMENTS.
COME, SIT DOWN AND RELAX! I KNOW THE FIRST DAY OF SCHOOL IS SO VERY HECTIC.
I'LL LEAVE YOU TO IT, PROFESSOR BARRENS.
OF COURSE.
WE HAVE MUCH WORK TO DO.
SO, WHAT KIND OF WORK AM I HELPING YOU WITH?
DON'T WORRY ABOUT THAT QUITE YET.
YOU WILL FEEL SO MUCH BETTER IF YOU HAVE SOME TEA FIRST.
I WOULD BE QUITE OFFENDED IF YOU TURN IT DOWN. I WORKED ALL WEEK ON THE RECIPE.

GO ON TO THE NEXT PAGE.

The professor stares at you expectantly.

WILL YOU . . .

. . . drink the tea?
TURN TO PAGE 58.

. . . try to leave the room?
TURN TO PAGE 69.

. . . spill the tea on purpose?
TURN TO PAGE 17.

As the ghost floats toward you, Jess gives you a frightened look. She yelps, "I'm out of here!" and turns and runs down the hallway. You stare at the ghost for a second before running after Jess.

"Wait!" The ghost floats up behind you. "I'm sorry I scared you," she says softly. "Most people just ignore me. I was hoping we could be friends . . ."

You smile at the spirit, surprised but relieved. "I could use another friend here, but . . . we should go check on Jess."

As you start down the hallway after Jess, the ghost floats beside you, telling stories about the secret passages and hidden rooms in the school. If Jess ever calms down again, she'll be so impressed by all this cool inside information, maybe she'll forget the fact that your new friend is a ghost . . .

THE END

You decide to pull the yellow switch. The wires rattle and shake as bright yellow bolts of electricity surge into the creature lying on the table. You hold your breath as the creature slowly opens its eyes.

As it sits up and looks around in confusion, it reminds you of a wild animal. Its eyes grow wide, and it leaps from the table and darts for the door to the lab. You chase after it, reaching the door just in time to see the thing run down the stairs toward the dorms.

You've released a monster into the school! If you don't get it back to the lab, you're probably going to get expelled . . . or maybe eaten.

Heading out of the lab, you try to think of where the creature might have gone.

GO ON TO THE NEXT PAGE.

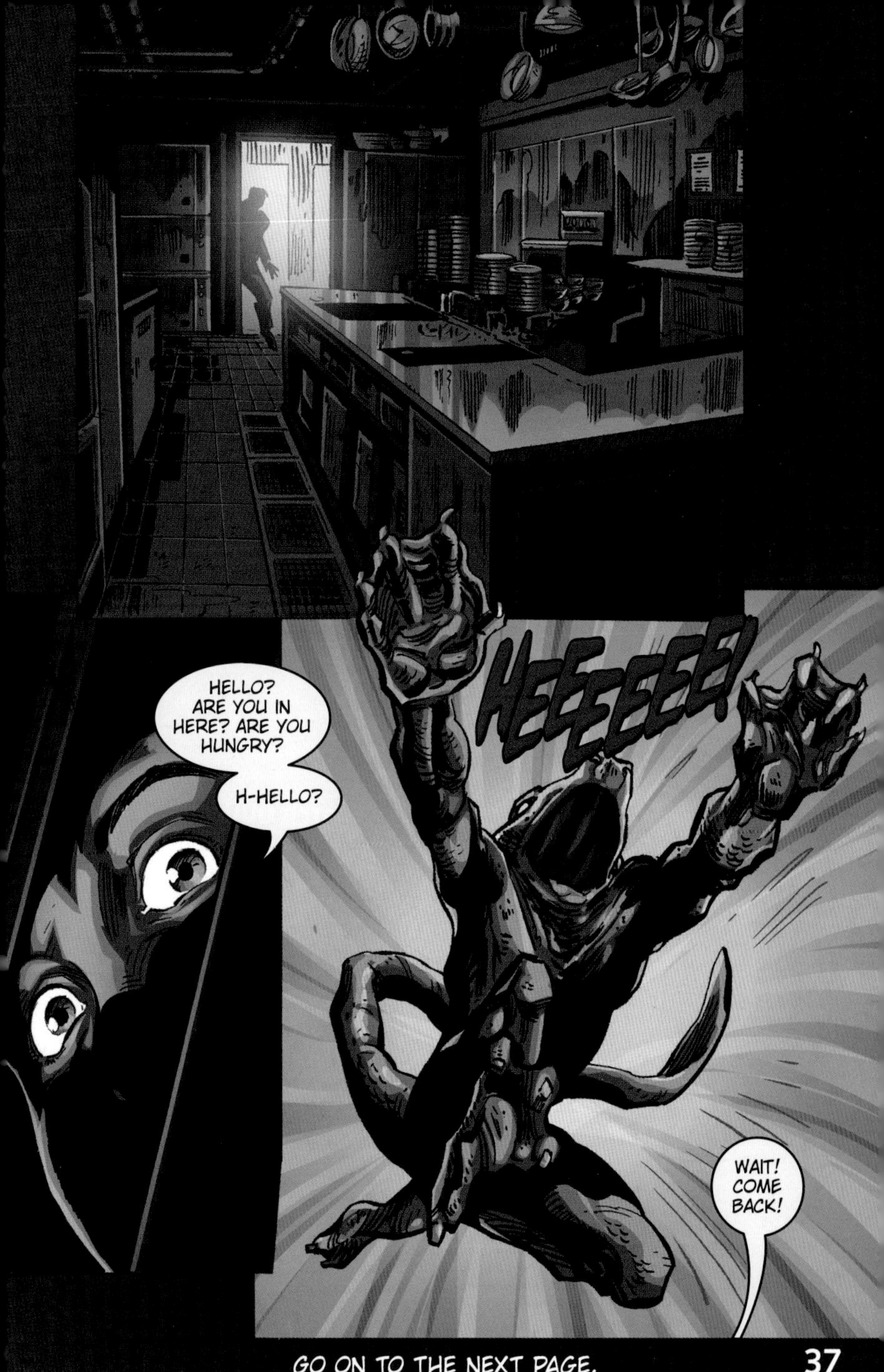
HELLO? ARE YOU IN HERE? ARE YOU HUNGRY?
H-HELLO?
HEEEEEEE!
WAIT! COME BACK!

If the creature has made it outside, you might never find it. But if it's still in the school, you have to find it before it wakes up the teachers. It could be anywhere!

WILL YOU . . .

. . . search the library?
TURN TO PAGE 30.

. . . search outside?
TURN TO PAGE 16.

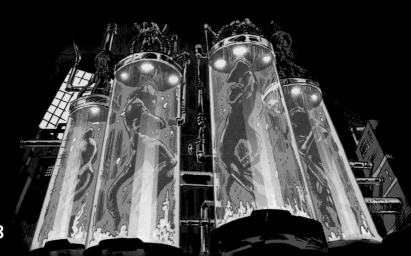

The headmaster smirks as he heads toward you. "Give us the book. Then I'll let you live." He stops right in front of you, waiting for your response.

You fling it out over the pool. The headmaster's face turns red as he screams in horror. "Nooooo!"

The two of you watch as the book hits the water and sinks beneath the surface. The headmaster wades into the water to try to retrieve it, but before he can reach it, one of the giant crocodiles leaps up and devours the book in one bite.

The headmaster quickly backs out of the water as the crocodile turns toward him. Seeing your opportunity to escape, you slip past, unnoticed by the reptiles.

Now all you have to do is locate Jess, escape from the teachers, and find your way out of the caverns. At least with that book gone, the worst they can do is assign you a lifetime of detention . . . right?

THE END

Turning to the left, you enter a room furnished as if a young girl lives there. The ghost floats through the room, moving through the bed to the closet.

She reaches through the closet door and moves her arms. She's mimicking pulling clothes out of the closet and holding them up as she searches for something to wear. Smiling, she floats over to the desk and tries to sit, hovering inches above the chair in an odd pantomime. She sits at the desk for a while, moving her hand as if writing something.

You watch her complete what looks like a daily routine. She finishes by standing and floating to the window, staring out at the school grounds below.

You step into the room, knowing that whatever the ghost wants is in here. The ghost spent a lot of time in the closet and at the desk. Maybe you should take a closer look at them.

GO ON TO THE NEXT PAGE.

WILL YOU . . .

. . . search the closet?
TURN TO PAGE 61.

. . . search the desk?
TURN TO PAGE 49.

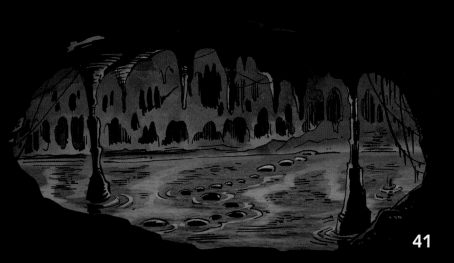

The spirit smiles and beckons to you as she turns and floats down the hallway. She leads the two of you far away from your dorms.

The spirit gestures at a door. Jess shrugs and leans close to the door, listening. "Hey, I think someone's crying."

You reach out and try the door. It takes both you and Jess to push it open. A small boy is sitting on the floor on the other side, shivering and scared. "I got lost!" he wails when he sees you. "I just wanted a drink of water, and then the door got stuck! I'm so glad you found me!"

You and Jess sit by the boy, calming him down until he's ready to walk back to the dorms.

The next morning, your teacher tells you that the student is okay, thanks to you and Jess. You smile, glad to have helped. You're also relieved that the spirit is there looking out for the students.

THE END

COME ON!

WOW! THIS REEKS. WHAT DO YOU THINK WAS IN IT?

ISN'T THIS WEIRD?

HEY, JESS, THERE'S ANOTHER DOOR HERE. LET'S KEEP MOVING BEFORE SOMEONE CATCHES US.

IT FEELS LIKE WE'RE NOT EVEN IN THE SCHOOL ANYMORE.

OH...

WHAT IS THIS PLACE?

GO ON TO THE NEXT PAGE.

43

You peer over the edge of the cliff and immediately wish you hadn't. The pool of water directly below you looks hard and black in the flickering light of the torches.

"Come on, let's check it out," Jess whispers.

"Then we'll go back to class?" you ask. You try to smile bravely at Jess, trying to ignore the creepy feeling you're getting.

She smiles back at you. "Yeah, but no swimming, right?" Both of you laugh at that, as you head down the steep path to the walkways that cut across the water below you.

At the bottom of the cliff, the narrow path branches in two. The right path leads across the lakes before disappearing into the dark cavern. The path right in front of you edges around the lake and into a tunnel.

"Which way do you want to go?" Jess asks in a whisper.

WILL YOU . . .

. . . cut across the lake?
TURN TO PAGE 54.

. . . walk around the edge and
down the tunnel?
TURN TO PAGE 74.

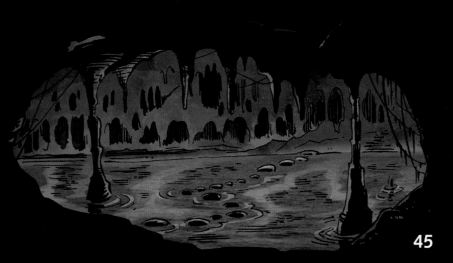

You shake your head. "No way. I want to figure out my regular classes before I start on any special projects."

Jess smiles brightly at you as she hops to her feet. "I'll tell you how it went later!" You wave at her as she follows another student out of the classroom.

Professor Aslem turns back to the class and resumes her lecture. No matter how hard you try to focus, as she drones on about the rules, you start daydreaming about the mysterious school. After what seems to be hours, the bell rings.

"This semester we will start with Mesopotamian mythology, and with some luck, we'll manage to get through the stories of Gilgamesh," Professor Aslem concludes. "Now, for tonight read chapters 1–7 in *Understanding Ancient Beliefs* and make a thorough outline. Class dismissed."

GO ON TO THE NEXT PAGE.

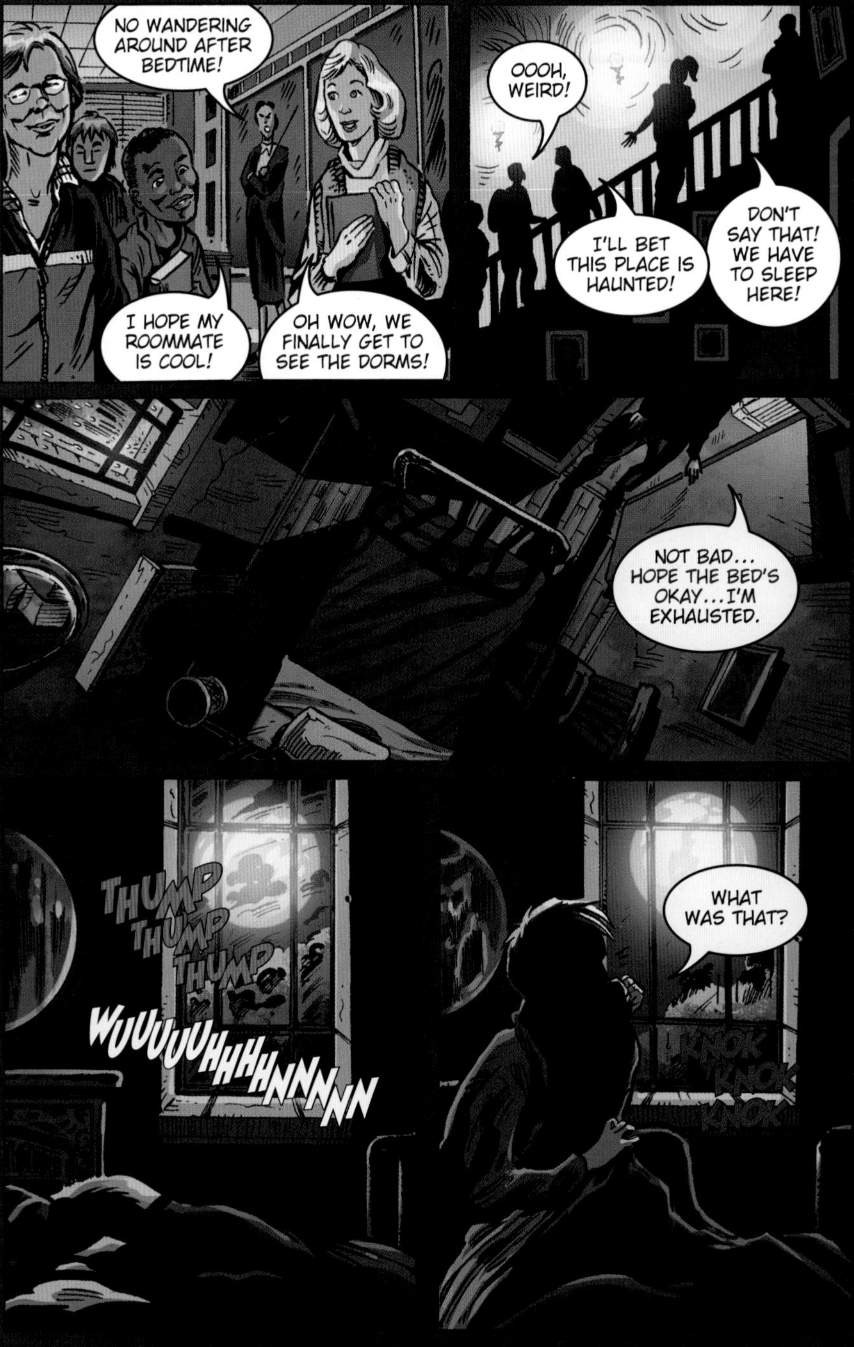
NO WANDERING AROUND AFTER BEDTIME!
I HOPE MY ROOMMATE IS COOL!
OH WOW, WE FINALLY GET TO SEE THE DORMS!
OOOH, WEIRD!
I'LL BET THIS PLACE IS HAUNTED!
DON'T SAY THAT! WE HAVE TO SLEEP HERE!
NOT BAD... HOPE THE BED'S OKAY... I'M EXHAUSTED.
THUMP THUMP THUMP
WUUUUUHHHHNNNNN
WHAT WAS THAT?
KNOK KNOK KNOK

GO ON TO THE NEXT PAGE.

Something about the mysterious knocking in the hallway sends chills down your spine.

WILL YOU . . .

. . . stay inside your room?
TURN TO PAGE 63.

. . . go investigate the hallway?
TURN TO PAGE 18.

The ghost spent more time at the desk, so you start your investigation there.

The old rolltop desk looks as if it were carved from one giant piece of dark wood. The handles on the drawers are ornately molded brass roses, still shiny and beautiful even after being ignored for years. Despite the age of the desk, the drawers open easily, revealing a lot of old textbooks and letters, note cards with black borders, and an old newspaper clipping.

You sit on the edge of the bed and begin to read through the letters. They were written to a female student who attended the school almost a century ago, and there are almost three years' worth. From what you can tell, she went by the nickname Sissy. Sissy loved the school dearly. The letters from her family and friends are all filled with happy news, until the last five.

GO ON TO THE NEXT PAGE.

THE LAST FIVE LETTERS ARE ABOUT SISSY'S LAST FEW MONTHS AT DARKHAM.

IN THE MIDDLE OF THE SCHOOL YEAR, SHE RECEIVED BAD NEWS FROM HOME.

HER GRANDMOTHER FELL ILL, AND SISSY'S MOTHER NEEDED SISSY TO RETURN HOME.

SISSY MUST HAVE BEEN DEVASTATED WHEN SHE FOUND OUT THAT SHE WOULD HAVE TO LEAVE HER BELOVED SCHOOL.

SISSY! YOUR FATHER'S HERE! HURRY UP.

GO ON TO THE NEXT PAGE.

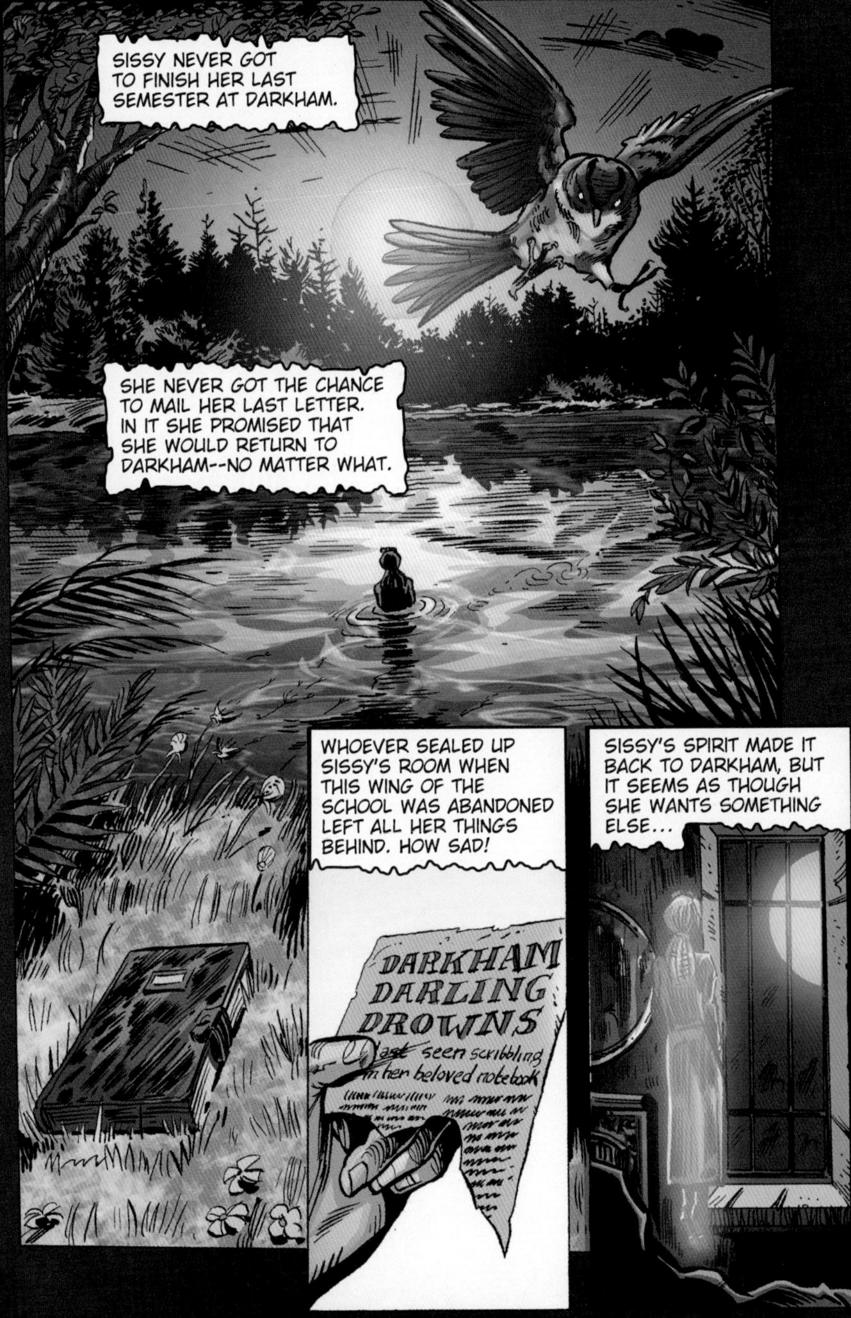
SISSY NEVER GOT TO FINISH HER LAST SEMESTER AT DARKHAM.
SHE NEVER GOT THE CHANCE TO MAIL HER LAST LETTER. IN IT SHE PROMISED THAT SHE WOULD RETURN TO DARKHAM--NO MATTER WHAT.
WHOEVER SEALED UP SISSY'S ROOM WHEN THIS WING OF THE SCHOOL WAS ABANDONED LEFT ALL HER THINGS BEHIND. HOW SAD!
DARKHAM DARLING DROWNS
last seen scribbling in her beloved notebook
SISSY'S SPIRIT MADE IT BACK TO DARKHAM, BUT IT SEEMS AS THOUGH SHE WANTS SOMETHING ELSE...

Sissy's spirit seems to be interested in something outside. Maybe you can do something to help her find peace. On the other hand, you've been out past curfew for a long time. Maybe you could help her during the day.

WILL YOU . . .

. . . help Sissy later?
TURN TO PAGE 65.

. . . help Sissy's spirit now?
TURN TO PAGE 100.

As Headmaster Malone walks closer, you grab the book and look around for a way to escape. The headmaster smiles down at you cruelly.

"Just give me the book," he says. "It will all be over soon."

Shaking your head furiously, you clutch the book tightly to your chest and run for the lake, pausing when you reach the edge of the lake. You look back at the headmaster long enough to see his face twist in shock and horror. As he runs toward you, you leap into the water.

It's colder than you expected, and the shock of it makes you drop the book. As you watch it sink to the bottom, you notice shadows circling you in the water. The creatures you saw earlier are closing in on you.

As they swim nearer, you have time to be glad that at least the book will be well guarded at the bottom of their lake.

THE END

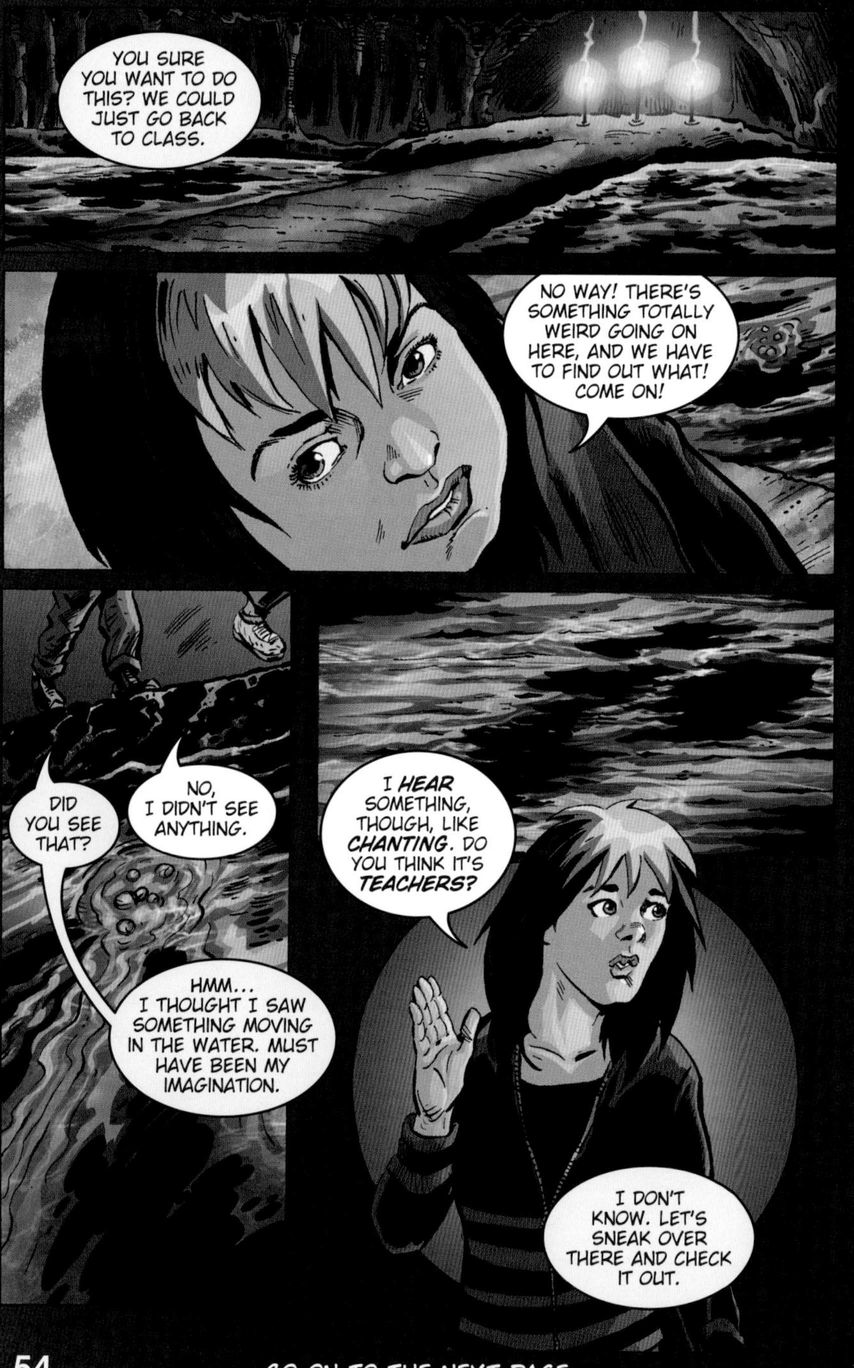

YOU SURE YOU WANT TO DO THIS? WE COULD JUST GO BACK TO CLASS.
NO WAY! THERE'S SOMETHING TOTALLY WEIRD GOING ON HERE, AND WE HAVE TO FIND OUT WHAT! COME ON!
DID YOU SEE THAT?
NO, I DIDN'T SEE ANYTHING.
HMM... I THOUGHT I SAW SOMETHING MOVING IN THE WATER. MUST HAVE BEEN MY IMAGINATION.
I *HEAR* SOMETHING, THOUGH, LIKE *CHANTING*. DO YOU THINK IT'S *TEACHERS?*
I DON'T KNOW. LET'S SNEAK OVER THERE AND CHECK IT OUT.

GO ON TO THE NEXT PAGE.

You and Jess tiptoe across the path leading into the cavern. Halfway across the lake, you can see that the shore on the far side is covered in large boulders. The chanting stops, but you think you hear something moving around.

As you step off the path onto the shore, a flickering light catches your eye. Grabbing Jess's hand, you dart behind one of the boulders and peer cautiously around it.

Rising out of the water is a large animal that's a cross between a giant squid and a crocodile. You and Jess gasp in horror as it turns its glowing red eyes to look at you. It moves faster than you thought it could as it lurches in your direction.

You feel pretty sure you and Jess could push one of the boulders onto the monster. But maybe it's better to outrun it across the narrow path.

GO ON TO THE NEXT PAGE.

The monster is charging!

WILL YOU . . .

. . . try to run?
TURN TO PAGE 15.

. . . push the boulder?
TURN TO PAGE 21.

Pulling the blankets over your head, you roll over and go back to sleep. After a while, you hear a knock at the door. Pulling yourself out of bed, you shuffle over to open the door.

Professor Aslem is standing at the door, scowling at you. "I trust you have a good reason for missing your second day of class."

You stare at your feet for a second as you try to think of a way to explain your absence. "I'm . . . sick?" you mutter, glancing up at the professor.

She glares at you suspiciously. "Very well. Just be sure to have chapters 8–14 completed for tomorrow. And since you have all this time on your hands, get a head start on chapters 15–25."

You realize that the hardest part of going to a boarding school will be dealing with the other people—not the ghosts. You head back to bed to try to get more sleep. You've got a long night of homework ahead of you.

THE END

Afraid of angering the professor, you pick up the cup and drink the thick liquid. It smells like fresh-cut grass and tastes like pureed spinach. And it's ice cold.

You put the cup down and look at the teacher. She smiles expectantly.

"Do you feel any different?" she asks. "Any . . . slimier?"

You start to answer, but your voice is thick and muffled. You raise your hands, only to realize that you don't have hands! Instead, you have thick, green pseudopods!

You look in the large mirror behind the professor. You barely recognize yourself. A large green slug is staring back at you.

The professor smiles. "How very helpful! That is the exact result I wanted."

You glare at the professor with your slug eyes, wondering if the change is temporary or permanent.

As Professor Barrens scoops you into a fish tank and drops in some leaves for your lunch, you think you might be here a very long while. At least you'll have plenty of time to figure out if slugs can call for help.

THE END

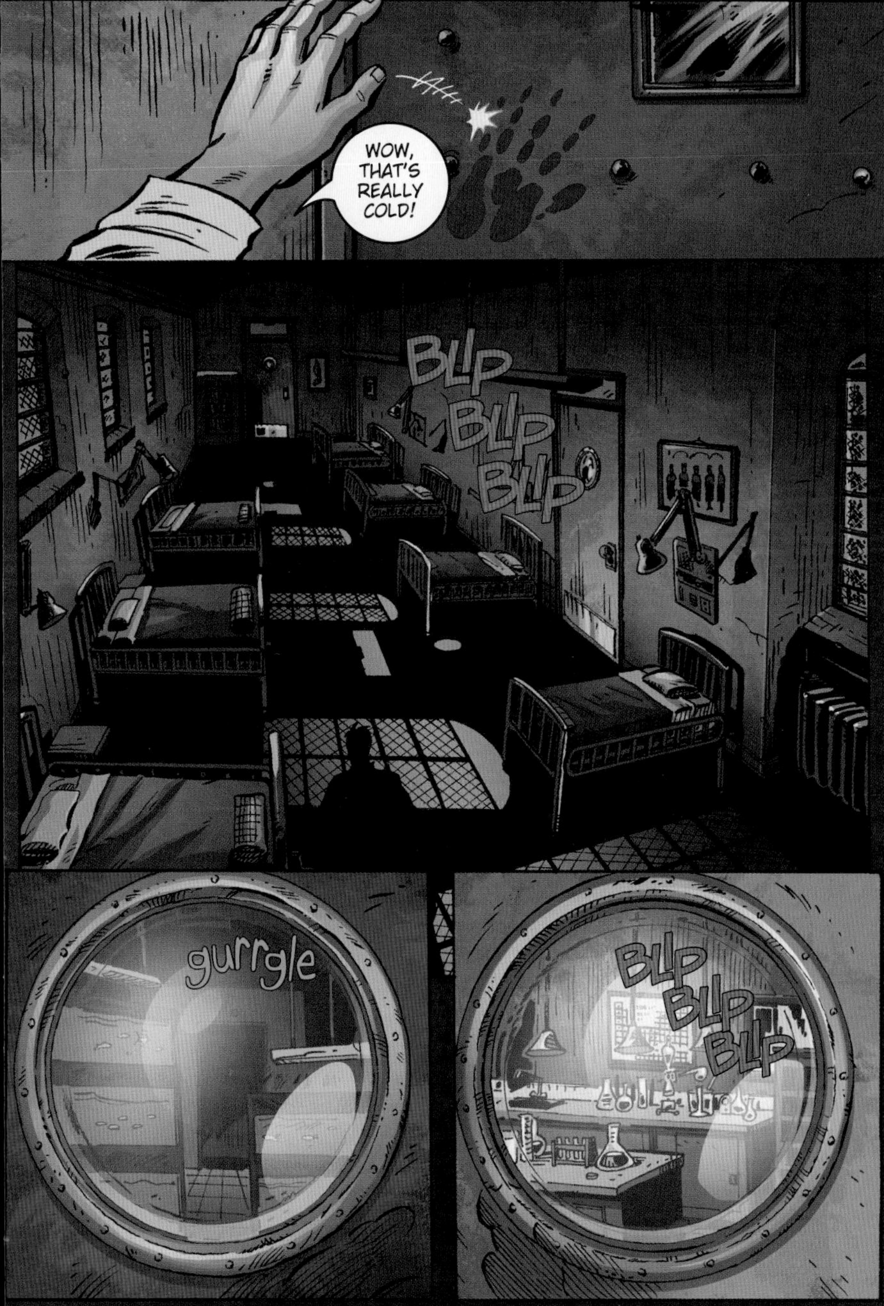
WOW, THAT'S REALLY COLD!
BLIP BLIP BLIP
gurrgle
BLIP BLIP BLIP

GO ON TO THE NEXT PAGE.

WILL YOU . . .

. . . go though the blue door?
TURN TO PAGE 66.

. . . investigate behind the chrome door?
TURN TO PAGE 88.

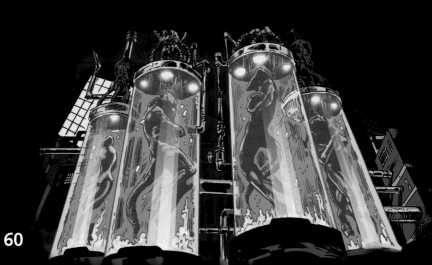

As you walk over to the closet, the ghostly girl vanishes from where she was standing by the window. She leaves nothing behind that would prove to anyone else that she was ever there.

For a brief moment, you wonder if she was real. Was your tired mind playing tricks on you? You smile at your nervousness and open the heavy closet door. Behind it is a large walk-in closet filled with silk dresses and shoes that look like they're hundreds of years old.

You dig through the clothes, looking for something that would be important to a spirit. Far in the back, close to the floor where most people would overlook it, you find a hidden door just big enough for you to squeeze through.

You push the panel open. On the other side is a dark passageway with a dim light at its end.

GO ON TO THE NEXT PAGE.

You crawl through the old-fashioned-looking clothes, shoes, and hats, hoping the tunnel goes somewhere interesting. After crawling forward for a minute or so, you'd be happy with somewhere boring too. Eventually the tunnel gets large enough for you to crouch and walk and then to stand up straight. That seems promising . . . you hope.

Although the tunnel has gotten bigger, it still feels cramped to you as you keep walking toward the light. It seems as though you've been walking for hours now, but the light hasn't gotten any brighter. Tired, you decide to give up and go back to your room.

Turning around, you see . . . the same light at the end of a long tunnel. No matter which direction you look, it's the same thing. You backtrack for what seems like forever, but the tunnel never changes. Finally, you realize the only solution is to sit down and wait for someone to find you. If they can.

Of course, you might literally be waiting forever . . .

THE END

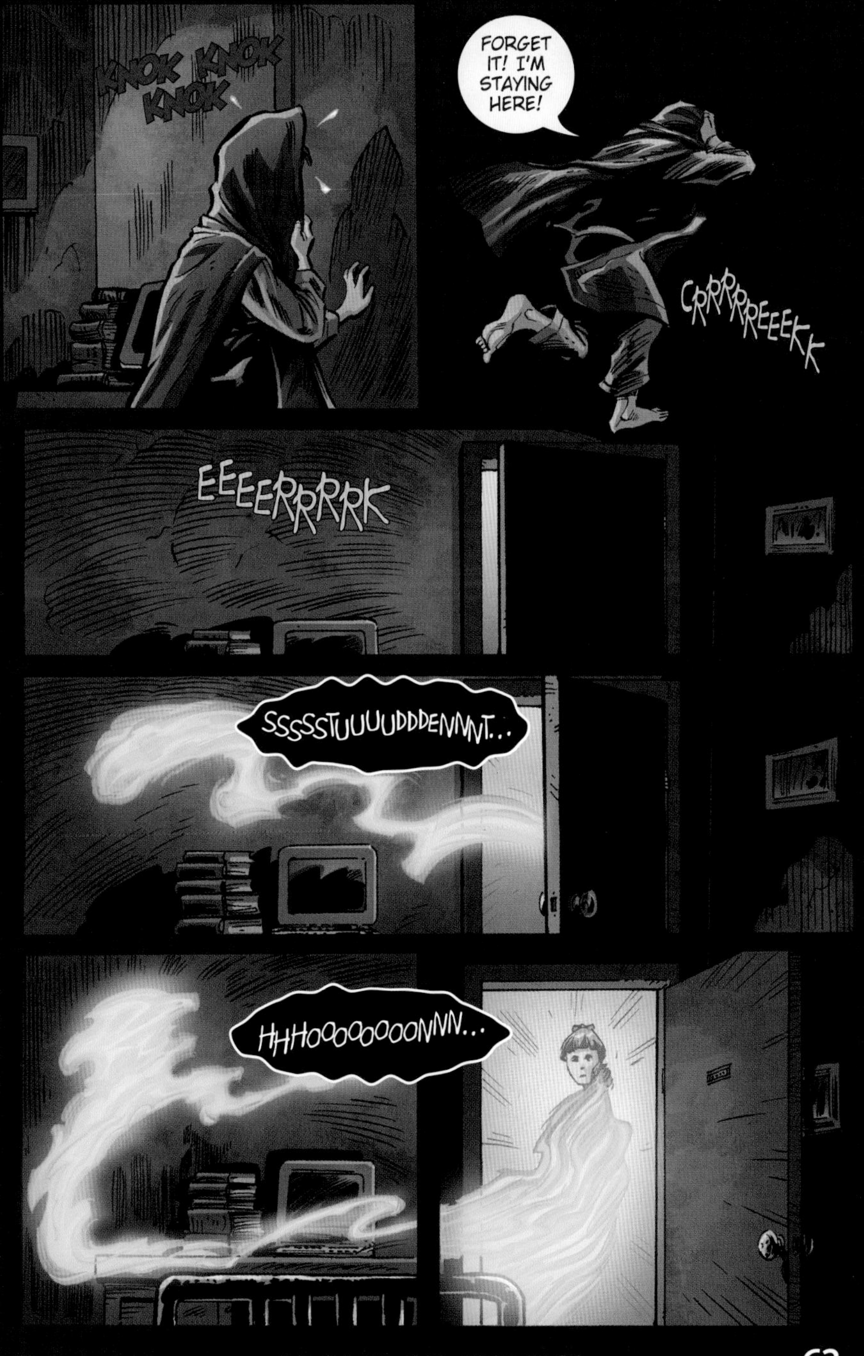
KNOK KNOK KNOK
FORGET IT! I'M STAYING HERE!
CRRRRREEEKK
EEEERRRRK
SSSSSTUUUUDDDENNNT...
HHHOOOOOOOONNN...

GO ON TO THE NEXT PAGE.

WILL YOU . . .

. . . confront the ghost?
TURN TO PAGE 72.

. . . run for the door?
TURN TO PAGE 96.

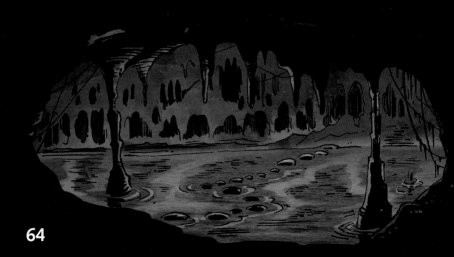

Deciding that staying out any later would be pushing your luck, you head back to your room for a good night's sleep.

You sleep well, and the next day passes uneventfully. But you are more anxious to get to bed than you've ever been. That night you lie awake waiting for the spirit to show up. You toss and turn all night, and as the sun rises, it finally occurs to you that she's not showing up.

The next night, you wait up again and the next, but the spirit never returns. When you think about it, you realize that you passed up the opportunity of a lifetime. The rest of your school year passes uneventfully . . . but the feeling that you missed out on something special never leaves you.

THE END

You push open the metallic blue door and find yourself standing in a large room filled with huge aquarium tanks. There are several large fish swimming in the tanks. As you look closely at them, you realize that they're not exactly fish. More like lizards with long, fishlike tails.

The pumps for regulating the water gurgle all around you. The underwater lights in the tanks give the whole room a greenish glow. At the far end of the lab, an open doorway leads to a pitch-black room. You can hear a loud splashing noise coming through the doorway.

You slowly approach the doorway, curious about what kind of fish the teachers are keeping in the back lab. You walk through the door, reaching out a hand to fumble around for a light switch.

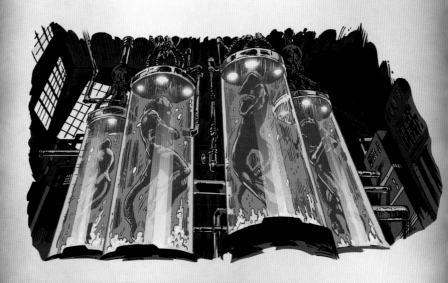

GO ON TO THE NEXT PAGE.

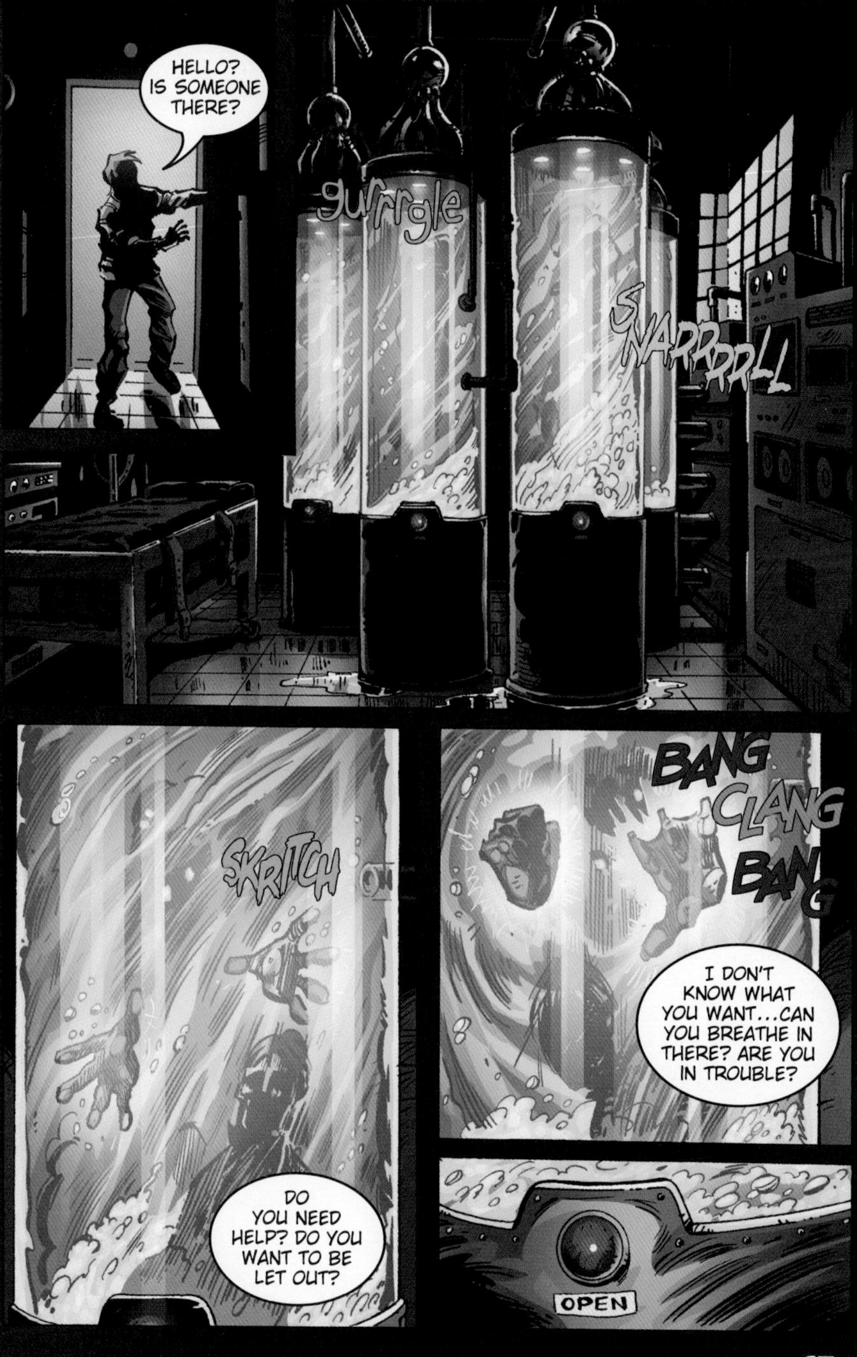
HELLO? IS SOMEONE THERE?
gurrrgle
SNARRRRLL
SKRITCH
BANG
CLANG
BANG
I DON'T KNOW WHAT YOU WANT...CAN YOU BREATHE IN THERE? ARE YOU IN TROUBLE?
DO YOU NEED HELP? DO YOU WANT TO BE LET OUT?
OPEN

GO ON TO THE NEXT PAGE.

TWISTED JOURNEYS®

The thing in the tank seems to want
something from you.

WILL YOU . . .

. . . press the red button and release the thing?

TURN TO PAGE 8.

. . . try to talk to it?

TURN TO PAGE 12.

You peer suspiciously at the murky cup as the teacher smiles at you. Deciding that the foul liquid isn't exactly your cup of tea, you push your chair back from the table.

"I'm allergic!" As you blurt out the first excuse that pops in your head, you can see the anger flicker across Professor Barrens's face. "Sorry," you continue, "I can't have any leaf-based foods." Before the teacher can say anything, you hurry out of the room.

Taking your seat back in the classroom, you wait for Jess. When she finally shows up, she is smiling mischievously.

"Did you drink the tea?" she asks. "I totally didn't! I told them my parents forbid me to drink hot beverages."

When you get back to class, the teacher has a surprising announcement: All first-year students have to take "etiquette classes" with Professor Barrens, to learn how to be polite when at a tea party.

Laughing quietly with Jess, you know that whatever weird plans the teachers have in store, the two of you can handle them.

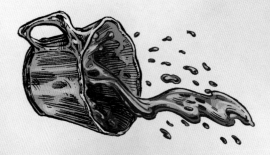

THE END

Stealing the book is too risky. You whisper, "Okay, let's try to get to the lever. If you cause a distraction, I think I can reach it."

Jess smiles at you. "I'm pretty good at creating a scene. When I start screaming, run."

You smile back at Jess. "Wish me luck."

Tiptoeing as silently as possibly, you sneak to the other side of the cavern, as the teachers begin chanting in the same strange language the headmaster was using.

Headmaster Malone throws his arms over his head. "Join us now, O ancient beast!"

You feel the ground shake, and a pungent fishy smell fills the room. The faint shape of a large twisted creature moves through the tunnel toward you.

Jess starts yelling at the top of her lungs. "Hey! Evil teachers! I know what you're doing!"

GO ON TO THE NEXT PAGE.

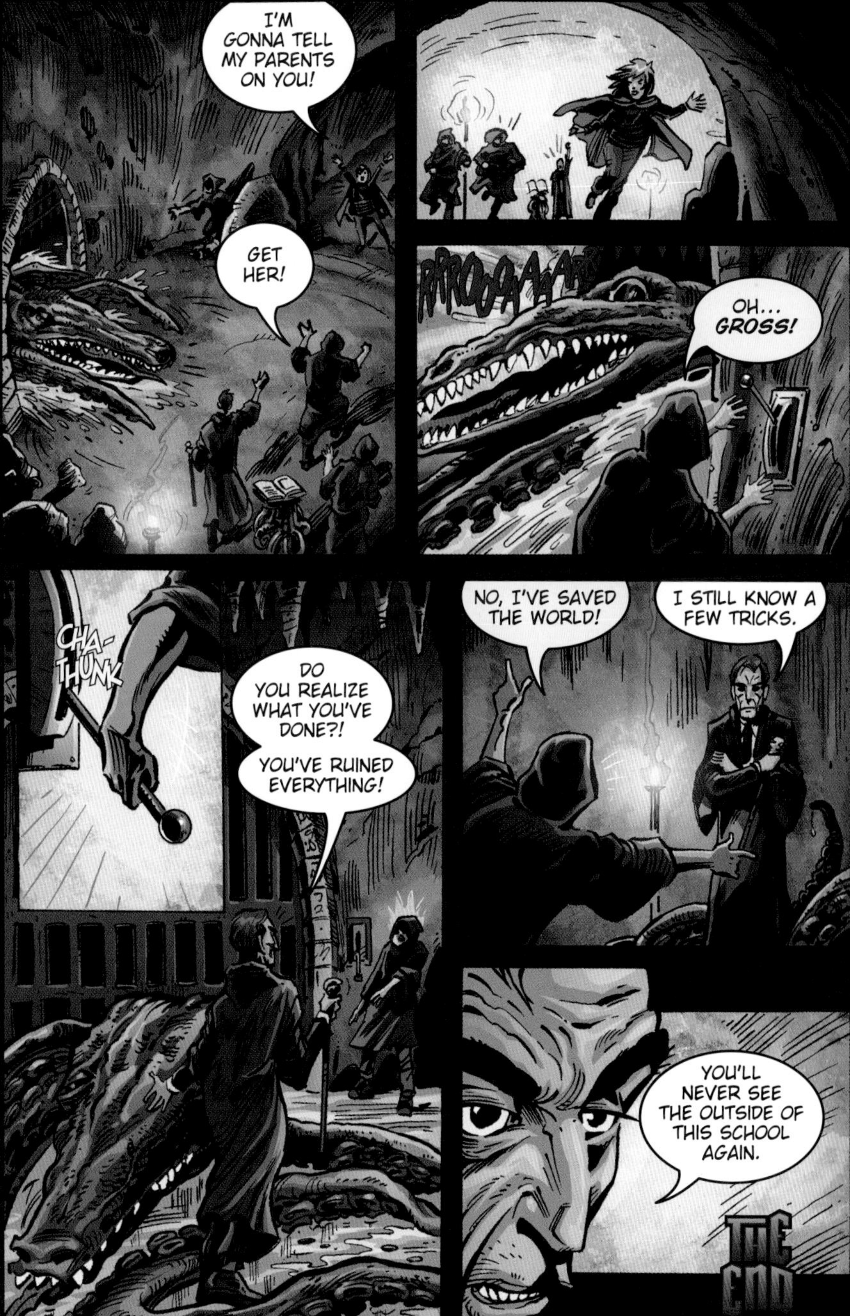
I'M GONNA TELL MY PARENTS ON YOU!
GET HER!
RRROOOAAAARR
OH... GROSS!
CHA-THUNK
DO YOU REALIZE WHAT YOU'VE DONE?!
YOU'VE RUINED EVERYTHING!
NO, I'VE SAVED THE WORLD!
I STILL KNOW A FEW TRICKS.
YOU'LL NEVER SEE THE OUTSIDE OF THIS SCHOOL AGAIN.
THE END

Taking a deep breath, you throw the blankets off your head and leap out of bed so you're standing face-to-face with the ghost. It pulls away from you, the surprise showing in its pale face and sunken eyes.

Taking advantage of its momentary pause, you try to sound brave as you ask, "Who are you? What are you doing here?" The spirit moans and stretches out its arm, gesturing for you to follow. Without waiting to see if you actually *are* following, the ghost floats out the door.

You watch the apparition float down the hall, heading into a part of the school you haven't seen yet. You slowly follow it to the end of the hall and to a large, dilapidated wooden door. The ghost turns to face you, still gesturing. You pause for a second, trying to decide if you want to follow the spirit.

GO ON TO THE NEXT PAGE.

This part of the school wasn't on the tour,
and following ghosts wasn't what
you had in mind tonight.

WILL YOU . . .

. . . follow the ghost?
TURN TO PAGE 85.

. . . attempt to
communicate with it?
TURN TO PAGE 31.

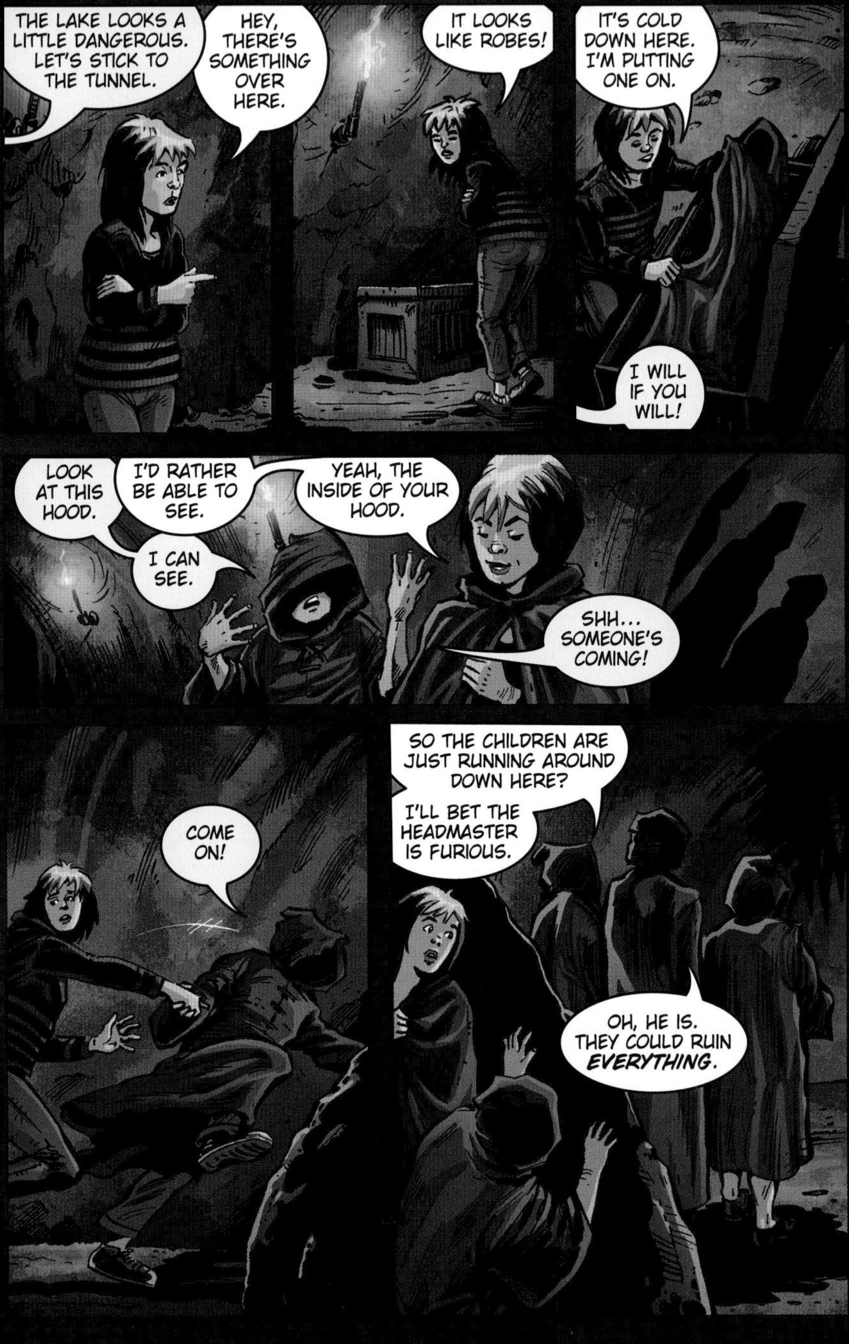
THE LAKE LOOKS A LITTLE DANGEROUS. LET'S STICK TO THE TUNNEL.
HEY, THERE'S SOMETHING OVER HERE.
IT LOOKS LIKE ROBES!
IT'S COLD DOWN HERE. I'M PUTTING ONE ON.
I WILL IF YOU WILL!
LOOK AT THIS HOOD.
I'D RATHER BE ABLE TO SEE.
I CAN SEE.
YEAH, THE INSIDE OF YOUR HOOD.
SHH... SOMEONE'S COMING!
COME ON!
SO THE CHILDREN ARE JUST RUNNING AROUND DOWN HERE?
I'LL BET THE HEADMASTER IS FURIOUS.
OH, HE IS. THEY COULD RUIN *EVERYTHING*.

GO ON TO THE NEXT PAGE.

You and Jess duck back behind the rock and wait for the teachers to walk out of earshot. Once they're gone, you climb out from behind the rock.

"What do you think we're about to ruin?" you whisper to Jess.

"I don't know," she replies. "Let's find out what they're doing!"

"Right. There's something bad going on here!"

The two of you creep quietly down the tunnel.

The tunnel opens into a broad, round room. A large, monstrous statue, some sort of creature with a dozen tentacles, hulks in front of a huge dark tunnel with a raised iron grate hanging from the entrance to the passageway. The teachers are walking calmly toward a hooded figure on the far side of the room, as if underground caverns with squid-monster statues are perfectly *normal*.

GO ON TO THE NEXT PAGE.

One of the teachers lowers the hood of his robe. Jess gasps and grabs your hand.

It's Headmaster Malone, with a huge leather-bound tome in his arms. Opening the book, he reads in a strange language as the teachers form a half circle in front of the statue.

"Now, with our final incantation, we will summon the vengeful Cephaloar from deep within the earth," the headmaster shouts, turning to face the tunnel, "to give us the unlimited dark powers we need to rule the world!"

You gasp at Jess, "Our teachers are evil! We've got to stop them!" You see a small lever next to the gate. "Look at *that*," you whisper. "We can get to the book, or we can try to shut the gate when this 'Cephaloar' comes through it."

"If we can grab the book, they can't summon him at all," Jess whispers back.

GO ON TO THE NEXT PAGE.

The teachers are completing their evil ritual.

WILL YOU . . .

. . . try to get across the room to the lever?
TURN TO PAGE 70.

. . . try to steal the book?
TURN TO PAGE 90.

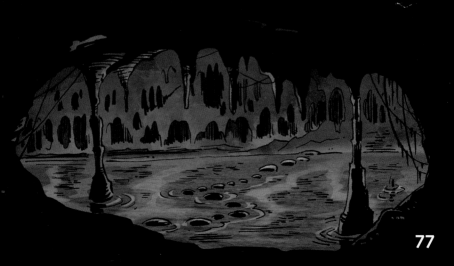

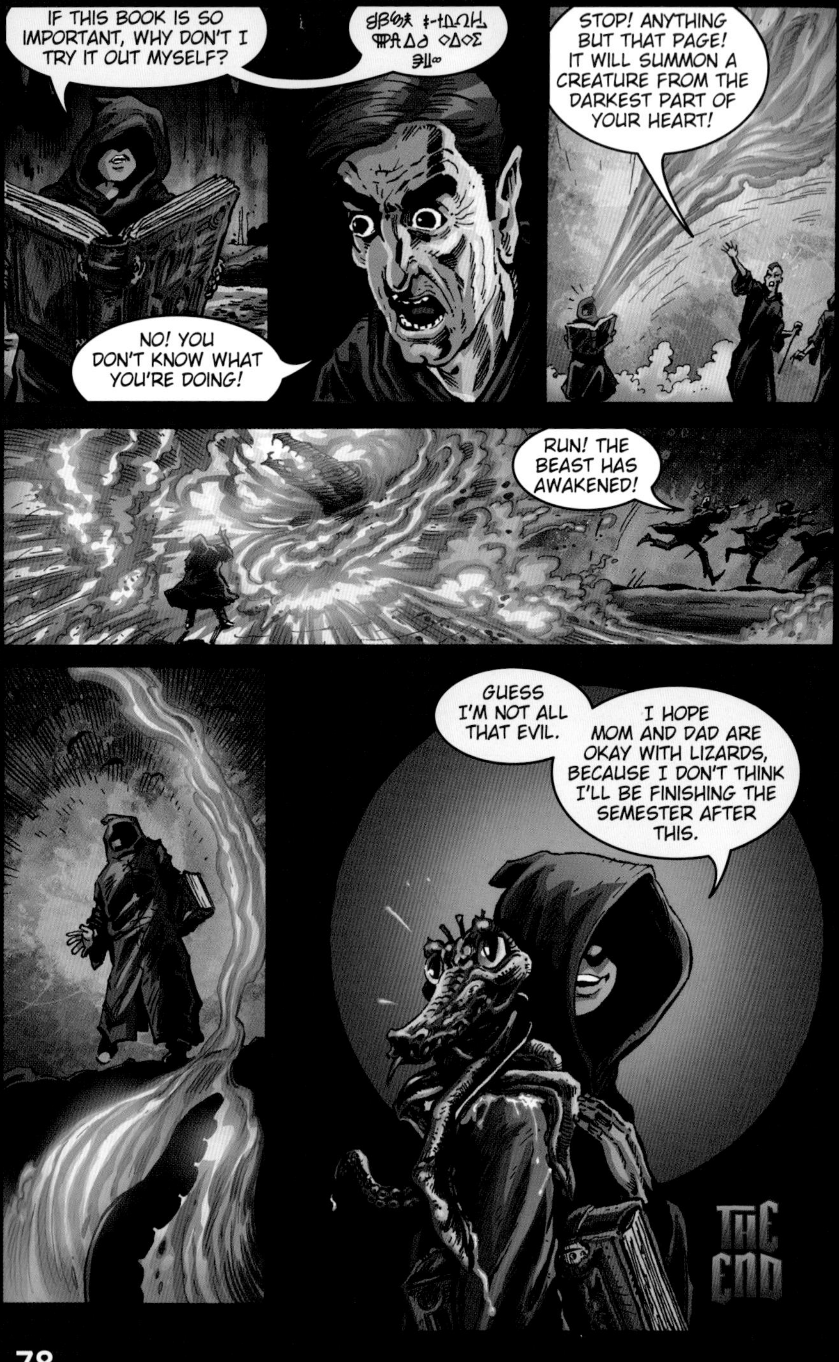
IF THIS BOOK IS SO IMPORTANT, WHY DON'T I TRY IT OUT MYSELF?
NO! YOU DON'T KNOW WHAT YOU'RE DOING!
STOP! ANYTHING BUT THAT PAGE! IT WILL SUMMON A CREATURE FROM THE DARKEST PART OF YOUR HEART!
RUN! THE BEAST HAS AWAKENED!
GUESS I'M NOT ALL THAT EVIL.
I HOPE MOM AND DAD ARE OKAY WITH LIZARDS, BECAUSE I DON'T THINK I'LL BE FINISHING THE SEMESTER AFTER THIS.
THE END

Rummaging through your strictest professor's classroom is the fastest way to get in massive trouble. You start searching the library first.

Pushing open the massive wooden door, you gasp at the size of the room. Floor-to-ceiling bookshelves line the walls, while dozens of smaller bookshelves are set up in tight lines across the room. In the middle of the room, there is a large glass case with a finely labeled plaque that reads "Our History."

In the case, there is a journal labeled "Sissy Craft," sitting on the top shelf. You hesitate as the ghostly image of Sissy reappears next to the case, looking down at the journal mournfully.

You take a deep breath and, grabbing the closest book, you smash open the case. Gingerly, you pick up the journal. You try to hand it to Sissy, but she drifts out of the library and pauses in the hallway.

Of course—how can a ghost carry a book? Maybe there's someplace you can take it for her.

GO ON TO THE NEXT PAGE.

You sit in the hallway and carefully open the old book. The smell of dust and centuries of old paper floats up from the pages. The ink has faded, but you can still make out Sissy's elegant handwriting. She describes the fun she had at Darkham, studying, hanging out with her friends, and making trouble for her teachers. As you read, you realize that she talks most of all about the river in back of the school.

In fact, the worse things got at home, the more she spent time at the river. She wrote that it was the only place where she felt like everything was still okay. Maybe Sissy's spirit will be at rest if you bring the book to the river.

You stand up, but before you're out the door, you hear footsteps. A teacher is headed your way!

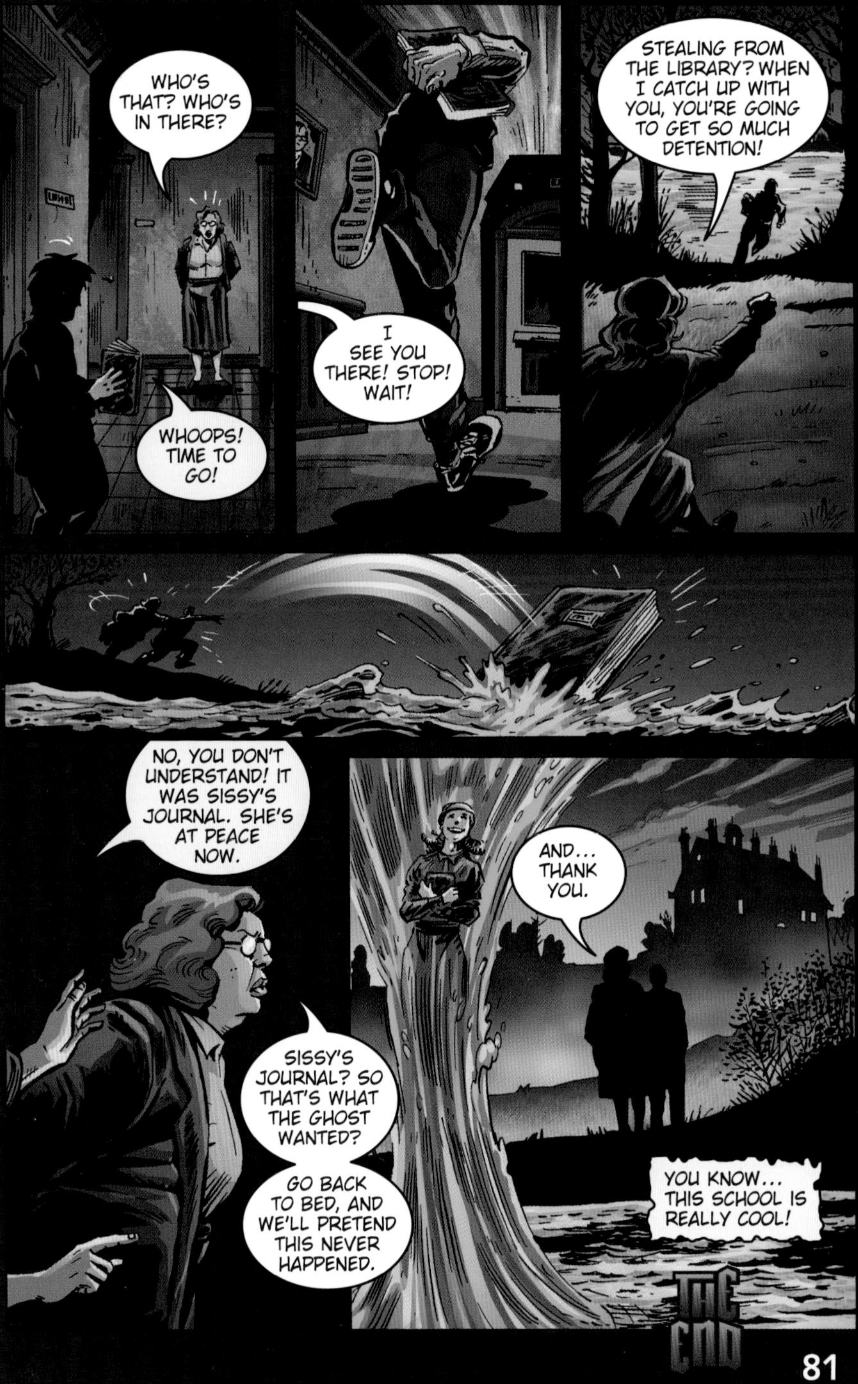
WHO'S THAT? WHO'S IN THERE?
WHOOPS! TIME TO GO!
I SEE YOU THERE! STOP! WAIT!
STEALING FROM THE LIBRARY? WHEN I CATCH UP WITH YOU, YOU'RE GOING TO GET SO MUCH DETENTION!
NO, YOU DON'T UNDERSTAND! IT WAS SISSY'S JOURNAL. SHE'S AT PEACE NOW.
SISSY'S JOURNAL? SO THAT'S WHAT THE GHOST WANTED?
GO BACK TO BED, AND WE'LL PRETEND THIS NEVER HAPPENED.
AND... THANK YOU.
YOU KNOW... THIS SCHOOL IS REALLY COOL!
THE END

At the bottom of the stairs, you head for the front door of the school. Out of the corner of your eye, you can see the ghost reaching out to grab you. You duck out of the way, and its hands pass harmlessly by, narrowly missing you.

You put on a burst of speed. You grab the handle of the door and fling it open as the ghost closes in on you again. You race down the stairs and turn to look at the school. The ghost hovers in the doorway, staring at you with its cold eyes.

You back away from the school, but the ghost stays in the door. Relieved that it isn't following, you turn your back on it and start the long walk toward town. Time to phone your parents and make them come and get you.

Weird teachers are one thing but going back to a haunted school—forget it!

THE END

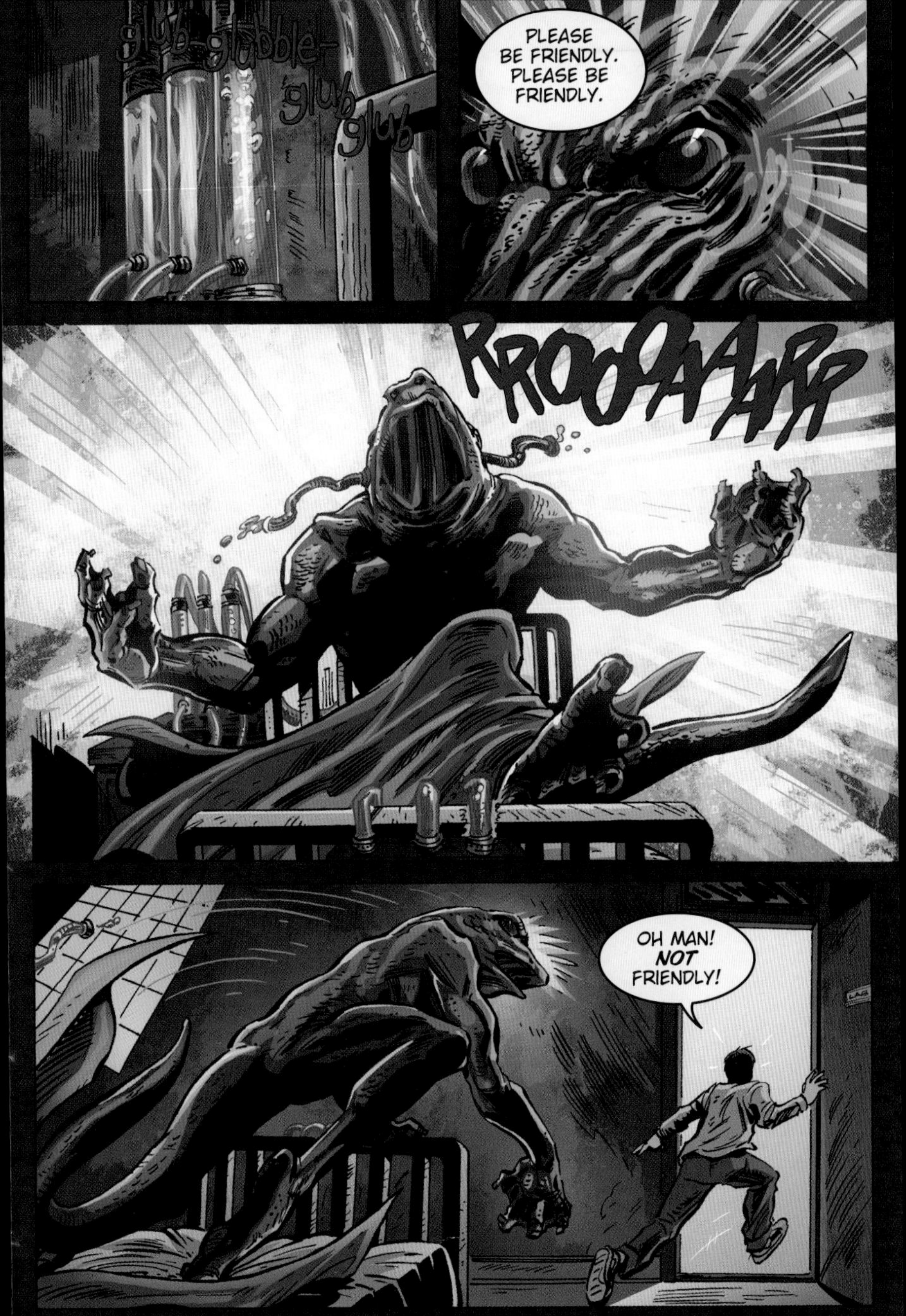
glub glubble-
glub glub
PLEASE BE FRIENDLY. PLEASE BE FRIENDLY.
RROOOAARR
OH MAN! *NOT* FRIENDLY!

The monster is hot on your heels! You'll have to do something to stop it, and you can only think of three places that could offer some kind of help.

WILL YOU . . .

. . . run to the dorms?
TURN TO PAGE 104.

. . . look for something that could help in the science labs?
TURN TO PAGE 98.

. . . go to the gymnasium?
TURN TO PAGE 93.

You follow the ghost through doorways and winding hallways of the school until you are no longer sure of where you are. This wing of the building looks much older than the areas you had previously seen.

The spirit guides you to a wooden staircase as ancient-looking as the rest of this wing. You slowly climb the stairs, listening to each board creak and pop as the ghost floats in front of you.

As you put your foot on the top stair, you hear a deafening snap, and the rotten wood gives out. You fall for a long time before landing hard on the floor.

As you rise to your feet, you realize that you are translucent, just like the spirit who is floating next to you, smiling happily. It looks like all it wanted was another ghost to be friends with . . . forever.

THE END

Even though you know you're going to get into trouble for being out past curfew, you know better than to approach a strange animal. You start to turn away from the aquarium slowly, but as you move, the creature lunges at the glass, cracking it.

You back away as the crack spreads from one side of the pane to the other. It's going to break right through at any moment. To your dismay, the creature inside the tank seems to know it's about to escape and smiles viciously at you. You turn and run for the door.

But you have to do something other than just run away, or the thing will be loose in the school. You race through the room, looking for a button or switch that will seal off the labs.

GO ON TO THE NEXT PAGE.

KRRRAAKK

COME ON! THERE'S GOT TO BE SOMETHING...

HA! THERE IT IS. I HOPE.

INNER SAFETY DOOR

KRRRAAKK klick

INNER SAFETY

WHIRRRRR

SAFETY DOOR DEPLOYED. INNER LAB SEALED.

THAT EXPLAINS WHY THEY TOLD YOU NOT TO GO WANDERING AROUND AT NIGHT. YOU'LL LISTEN TO YOUR TEACHERS FROM NOW ON!

THE END

The chrome door feels cold, and you shiver as you push it open. You're determined to track down the sounds you were hearing.

In the middle of the room sits a large bed. Lying on it is a bizarre creature with a humanlike body covered in scales and a ferocious lizard head. As you slowly approach the bed, you realize that the creature is frowning and growling slightly in its sleep.

You look around the rest of the room. At the foot of the bed, there are three switches, each connected to a different colored tube. The green tube is labeled "inquisitive," the yellow one is marked "moderate," and the red one has a tag that says "active." The tubes are connected to the creature's head. After studying the switches, you think they must somehow be related to the creature's mood.

GO ON TO THE NEXT PAGE.

WILL YOU . . .

. . . flip the green switch?
TURN TO PAGE 108.

. . . flip the yellow switch?
TURN TO PAGE 36.

. . . flip the red switch?
TURN TO PAGE 83.

. . . go back and try the other door?
TURN TO PAGE 66.

ONE OF US NEEDS TO CREATE A DIVERSION. IF YOU CAN GET THEM AWAY FROM THE BOOK, I'LL GRAB IT AND RUN.

YEAH, I'M PRETTY GOOD AT GETTING ATTENTION.

GOOD LUCK.

I DON'T NEED LUCK. I TOOK TRACK!

OOPS! HOPE YOU DIDN'T NEED THAT.

GO ON TO THE NEXT PAGE.

Jess grins at the teachers and then turns and runs out with them close behind her. You push yourself back against the wall as they run past you. After they chase her down the hallway, you sneak into the room.

The mysterious tome is lying on the floor where the headmaster dropped it when he ran after Jess. You grab the book and run, looking for somewhere to hide before the teachers return.

You make it back to the path across the lake, but the teachers and the headmaster are heading your way. "I can't believe we lost her," one of them is muttering. "Where—hey!" All the teachers look up and see you.

Headmaster Malone steps forward and glares at you. "And what are you planning to do with that book?"

GO ON TO THE NEXT PAGE.

WILL YOU . . .

. . . confront the headmaster?
TURN TO PAGE 10.

. . . escape across the lake?
TURN TO PAGE 26.

As the creature struggles to get off the table, you turn and run toward the gymnasium. You weave through the maze of dorm hallways to confuse the monster and buy yourself some time as you try to come up with a plan. You haven't seen the gym yet, but you're pretty sure that it will at least have a couple of baseball bats.

You reach the gym door and push it open. It turns out the school has an Olympic-quality training facility, with basketball courts, trampolines, and other gymnastic equipment. Against the back wall, between the two locker room doors, there is a rack of every kind of ball imaginable and a couple of badminton nets.

More than enough to make a trap.

GO ON TO THE NEXT PAGE.

WHEW...
JUST IN
TIME.

ZIIIIIP

THUD THUD
THUD

THUMP

THUMP

BOP

MUH?

94

GO ON TO THE NEXT PAGE.

The creature growls and struggles . . . but he can't break loose!

You sigh in relief. The creature is secured. Now the only things left to do are to drag him back to his lab and then explain everything to Headmaster Malone.

At least *he's* not a lizard-monster!

THE END

You lie under the blankets watching the ghost float around your room. It seems to be searching for something . . . or someone. When its back is turned, you throw your blankets off and dash for the door, running as fast as you can. When you get to the stairs, you look over your shoulder. The ghost is following right behind you, arms outstretched.

You speed up as you run down the stairs, taking them two at a time, but you can't escape from the ghost. Before you reach the bottom of the stairs, you feel an icy wind on the back of your neck. You know the spirit is catching up to you.

The stairs end in a hallway that stretches off in two directions. To the left, the hallway leads to the classrooms. The right leads out the front door of the school. The ghost is right behind you!

GO ON TO THE NEXT PAGE.

A light is on in one of the classrooms, but the door to the outside is closer.

WILL YOU . . .

. . . run for the front door of the school?
TURN TO PAGE 82.

. . . head to the classrooms to try to find a teacher?
TURN TO PAGE 107.

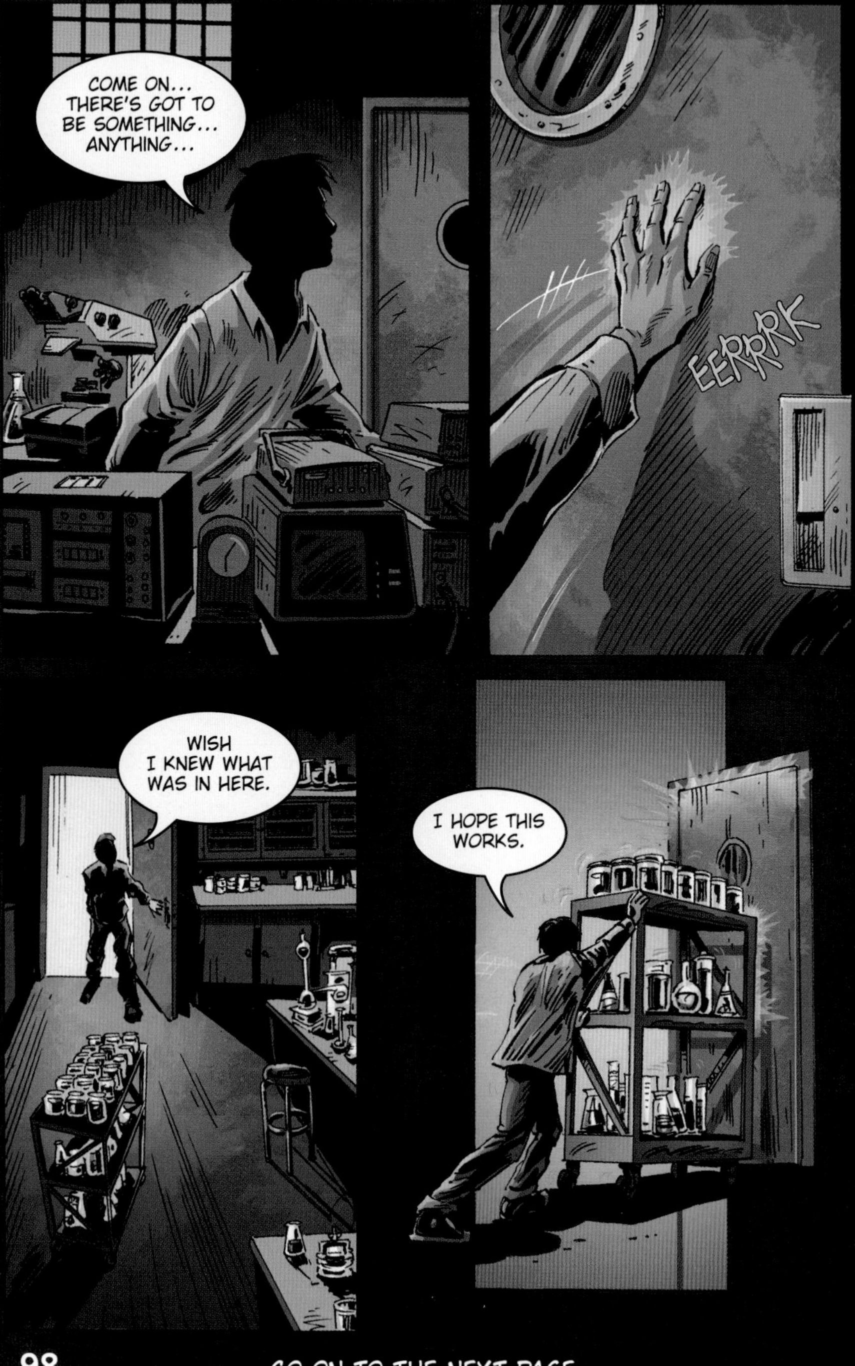
COME ON... THERE'S GOT TO BE SOMETHING... ANYTHING...
EERRRK
WISH I KNEW WHAT WAS IN HERE.
I HOPE THIS WORKS.

GO ON TO THE NEXT PAGE.

You wrestle the rack into place, leaning it against the door, hoping that when the monster pulls the door open it will topple over on him. With any luck, whatever the chemicals are in the unlabeled jars will help stop him too.

With the rack in place, you crouch in the corner of the room, waiting and listening.

The monster slowly pushes the door open and, as you planned, the rack topples over on the creature. A thick green cloud rises from the chemicals, and you start to grow sleepy as you breathe it in. Oh, boy—maybe mixing unfamiliar chemicals wasn't a smart idea. You should've paid more attention in chemistry class.

Right before you pass out, you hope the effects of the gas aren't permanent . . . and that you wake up before that monster does!

THE END

Sissy's story is too sad to ignore. You decide to help her immediately. Walking over to the window, you see that it looks out onto the river she mentioned in her letters.

You read over the newspaper clipping again. Sissy was last seen writing in her journal, and she talked about it a lot in her letters. Ghosts sometimes go looking for lost things, don't they? It's a long shot, but if you find a way to get the journal back to her, maybe her spirit will stop haunting the school.

Finding a single book in a school won't be an easy task. It could be in the library or in one of the classrooms. It could even still be by the river, completely ruined after all these years.

You vaguely remember seeing a thick, leather-bound book that matches Sissy's description of her journal on Professor Aslem's desk. But getting caught sneaking into a classroom after lights-out might be worse trouble than putting up with a ghost for the rest of the semester.

GO ON TO THE NEXT PAGE.

The library will take longer to search, but there's less of a chance that any teachers will be there this late.

WILL YOU . . .

. . . search the library?
TURN TO PAGE 79.

. . . search the professor's classroom and risk getting caught?
TURN TO PAGE 103.

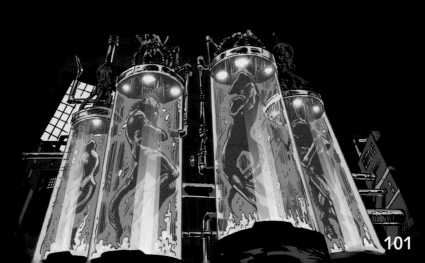

You back away from Headmaster Malone until you hit the stone wall of the cavern.

The headmaster smiles down at you wickedly. "There's simply nowhere for you to run. Give us the book, and I promise you'll survive." You sigh, defeated.

Dropping the book at the old man's feet, you bow your head. The headmaster quickly grabs the book and opens it. He begins to read the strange words inside. You stare in horror as green mist swiftly fills the cavern. Headmaster Malone laughs as the mist solidifies into a huge reptilian beast.

"The destroyer has come!" he shouts in pure delight. "It will destroy everyone who opposes me, and I will rule over all!" As the beast marches through the caverns toward the school, you wish you had done anything else but give the book to the headmaster. Rolling out of the monster's reach, you leap to your feet and try to run, but when you put any pressure on your foot, pain shoots up your leg. You must have injured it falling down the stairs. Looking over your shoulder, you see the monster shambling toward you and you know that you have to keep moving.

THE END

NOTHING HERE...

...OR HERE...

...OR HERE, EITHER. MAYBE THIS WAS A BAD IDEA.

IS SOMEONE IN THERE?

OH NO--I'M TRAPPED!

WHAT ARE YOU DOING HERE!

I WAS LOOKING FOR A BOOK.

SURE YOU WERE. YOU'LL HAVE PLENTY OF TIME TO READ IN DETENTION.

BUT-- I NEED--

OH WELL. MAYBE IN DETENTION YOU'LL HAVE TIME TO FIGURE OUT HOW TO HELP SISSY.

THE END

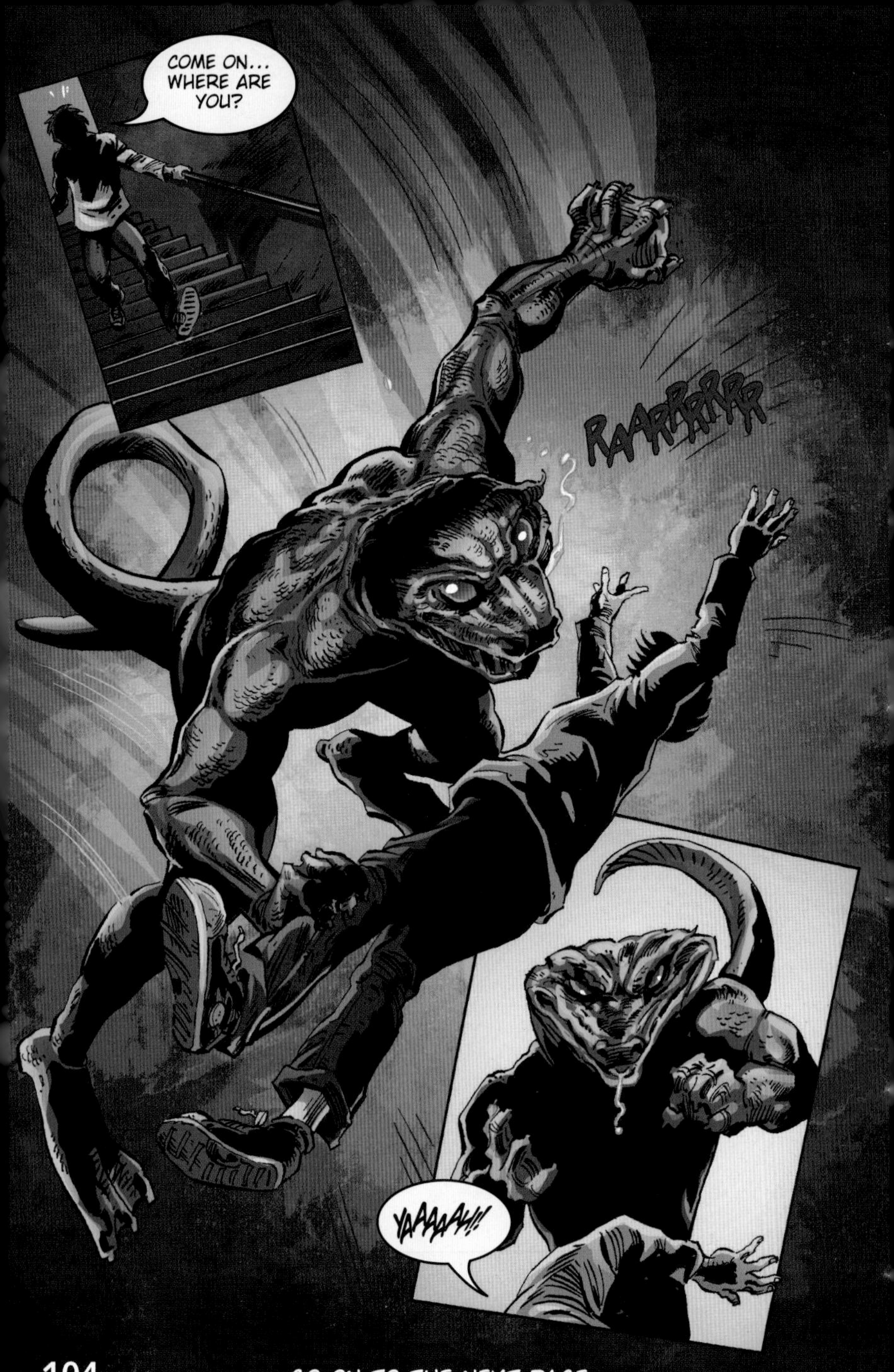
COME ON... WHERE ARE YOU?
RAARRRRRR
YAAAAAH!!

GO ON TO THE NEXT PAGE.

Limping, you head for the dorms, the monster hot on your heels. You grit your teeth in determination and ignore the pain. Finally, you round the corner and see the long line of dorm room doors.

You fall against the first door, banging on it with both fists as hard as you can. After what seems like forever, Jess pulls the door open. "What's going on? It's late!" Out of breath, all you can do is point at the monster coming up behind you.

GO ON TO THE NEXT PAGE.

Jess's eyes open wide as she sees the monster for the first time. "What is that?!"

You barely manage to gasp out the word, "Help!" Anyone else would have slammed the door in your face, but adventurous Jess runs down the hall knocking on every door, screaming, "Help! Monster!"

The other students emerge from their rooms, rubbing their eyes in the light. But their sleepiness disappears at once as they see the creature coming toward them. With your last bit of strength, you point at the monster: "We've got to stop it!"

The students form a circle around the creature. Outnumbered and confused, it roars angrily. One of the older kids jumps on its back and brings it to its knees. The other students jump on the beast and hold it down until help arrives.

When it's all finally over, everyone turns to you, full of questions. You tell them the whole story. But you know the best part of it is the ending—the heroics of your fellow students.

THE END

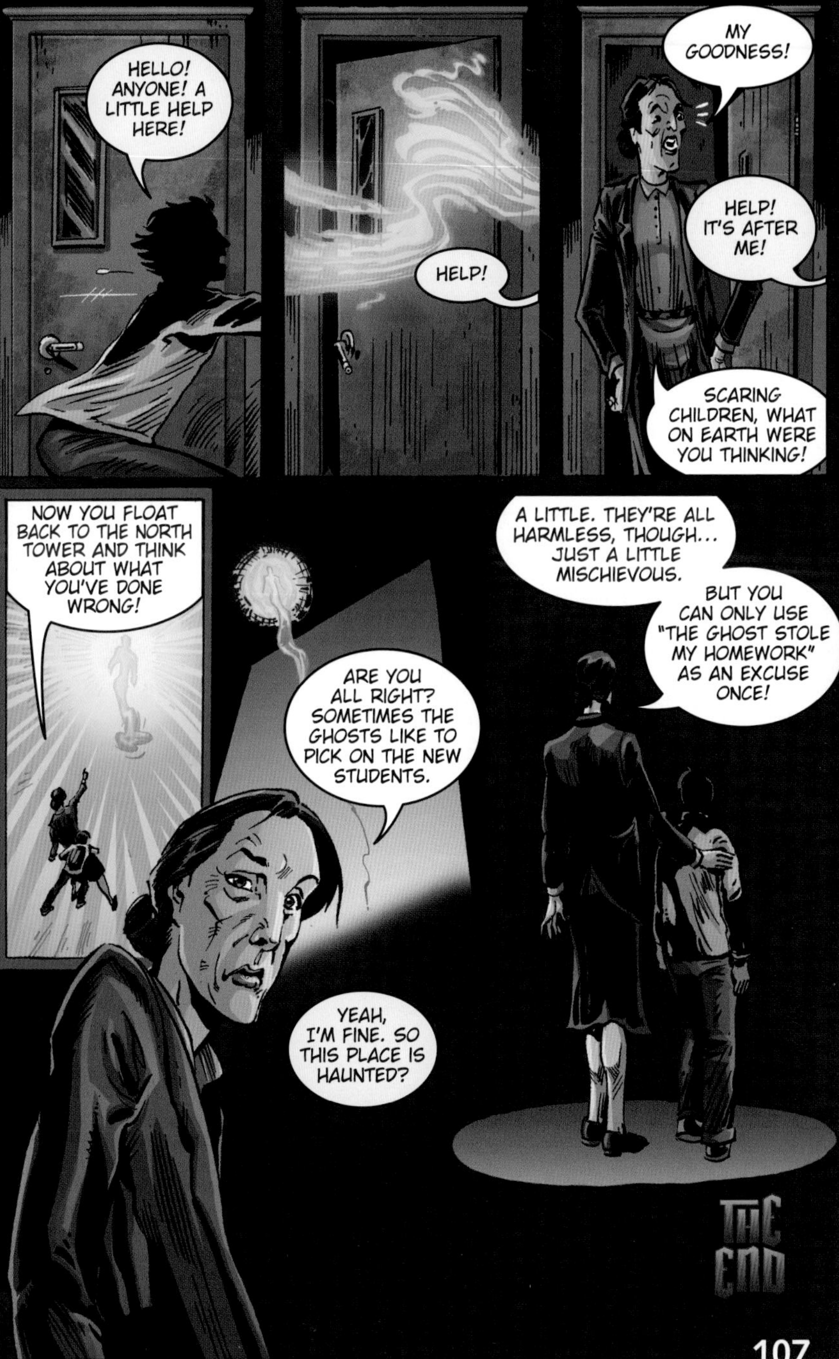
HELLO! ANYONE! A LITTLE HELP HERE!
HELP!
MY GOODNESS!
HELP! IT'S AFTER ME!
SCARING CHILDREN, WHAT ON EARTH WERE YOU THINKING!
NOW YOU FLOAT BACK TO THE NORTH TOWER AND THINK ABOUT WHAT YOU'VE DONE WRONG!
ARE YOU ALL RIGHT? SOMETIMES THE GHOSTS LIKE TO PICK ON THE NEW STUDENTS.
YEAH, I'M FINE. SO THIS PLACE IS HAUNTED?
A LITTLE. THEY'RE ALL HARMLESS, THOUGH... JUST A LITTLE MISCHIEVOUS.
BUT YOU CAN ONLY USE "THE GHOST STOLE MY HOMEWORK" AS AN EXCUSE ONCE!
THE END

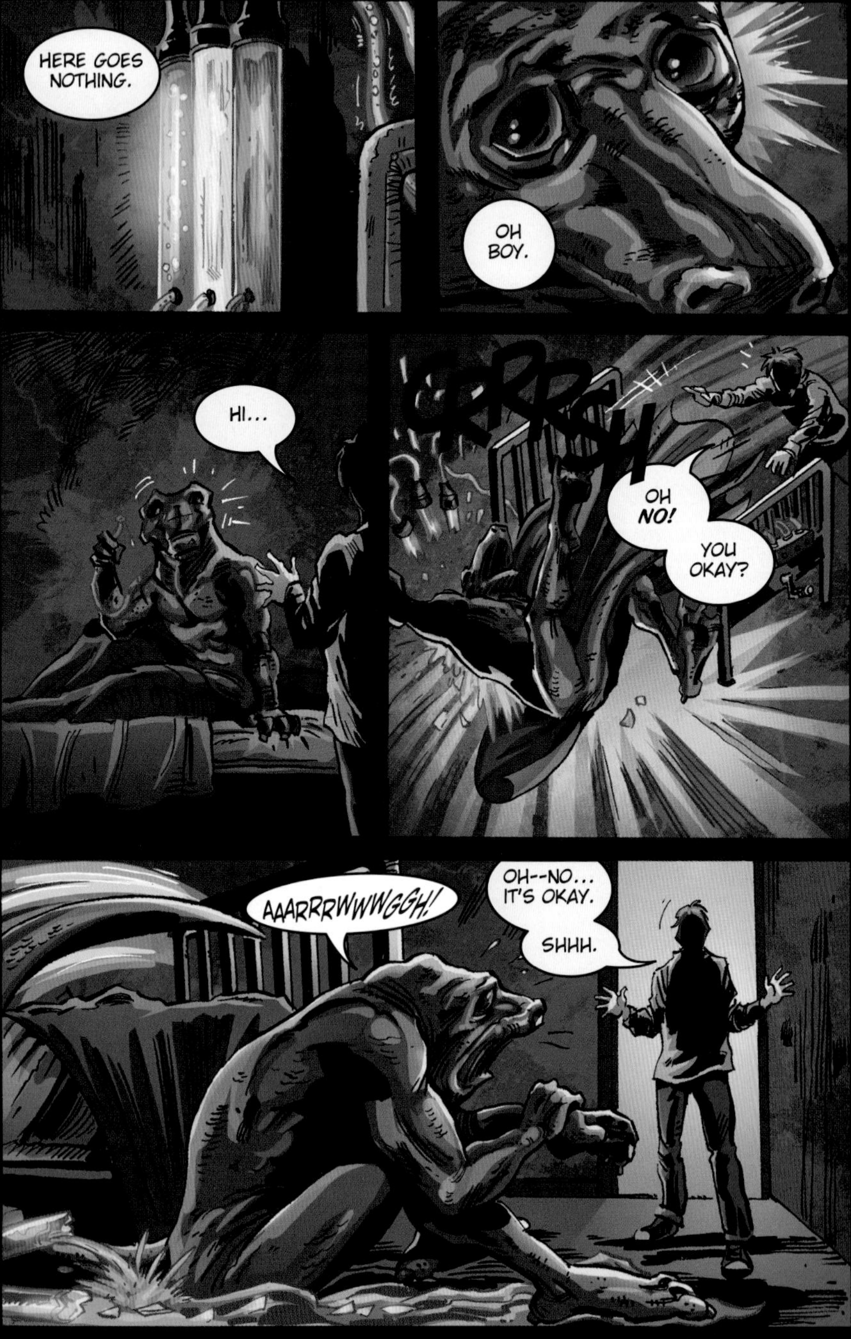
HERE GOES NOTHING.
OH BOY.
HI...
CRRRSH
OH NO!
YOU OKAY?
AAARRRWWWGGH!
OH--NO... IT'S OKAY.
SHHH.

GO ON TO THE NEXT PAGE.

The monster howls again in pain as it slowly moves across the lab, holding one injured hand with the other and limping on its left leg. The sound reverberates around the room, loud enough to alert the teachers.

You've got to get this poor, tormented animal out of the lab, so it can be free from whatever experiments they were subjecting him to. Ripping the sleeve off your shirt, you move toward the creature to bandage its wound. It looks up at you suspiciously, but as you talk calmly to it, the lizard allows you to bandage it.

As you finish wrapping its hand, the lizard jerks its head toward the door. You can hear footsteps approaching. If you're going to get the lizard out of the school, you have to go now.

GO ON TO THE NEXT PAGE.

You grab the creature's hand and make your way to the door, peering out to check to make sure the coast is clear. You can hear the footsteps coming toward you from the hallway.

You realize if you're going to get away, you have to head deeper into the lab. You point toward the door across the hall from you, gesturing to the lizard. "Go!" you whisper.

You follow behind the lizard as it sprints across the hall, but just as you reach the door, you see a teacher turn the corner.

"Hey!" You hear the teacher shout as you barrel through the door into a room lined with aquariums filled with smaller, normal lizards.

The creature races for a door in the back.

GO ON TO THE NEXT PAGE.

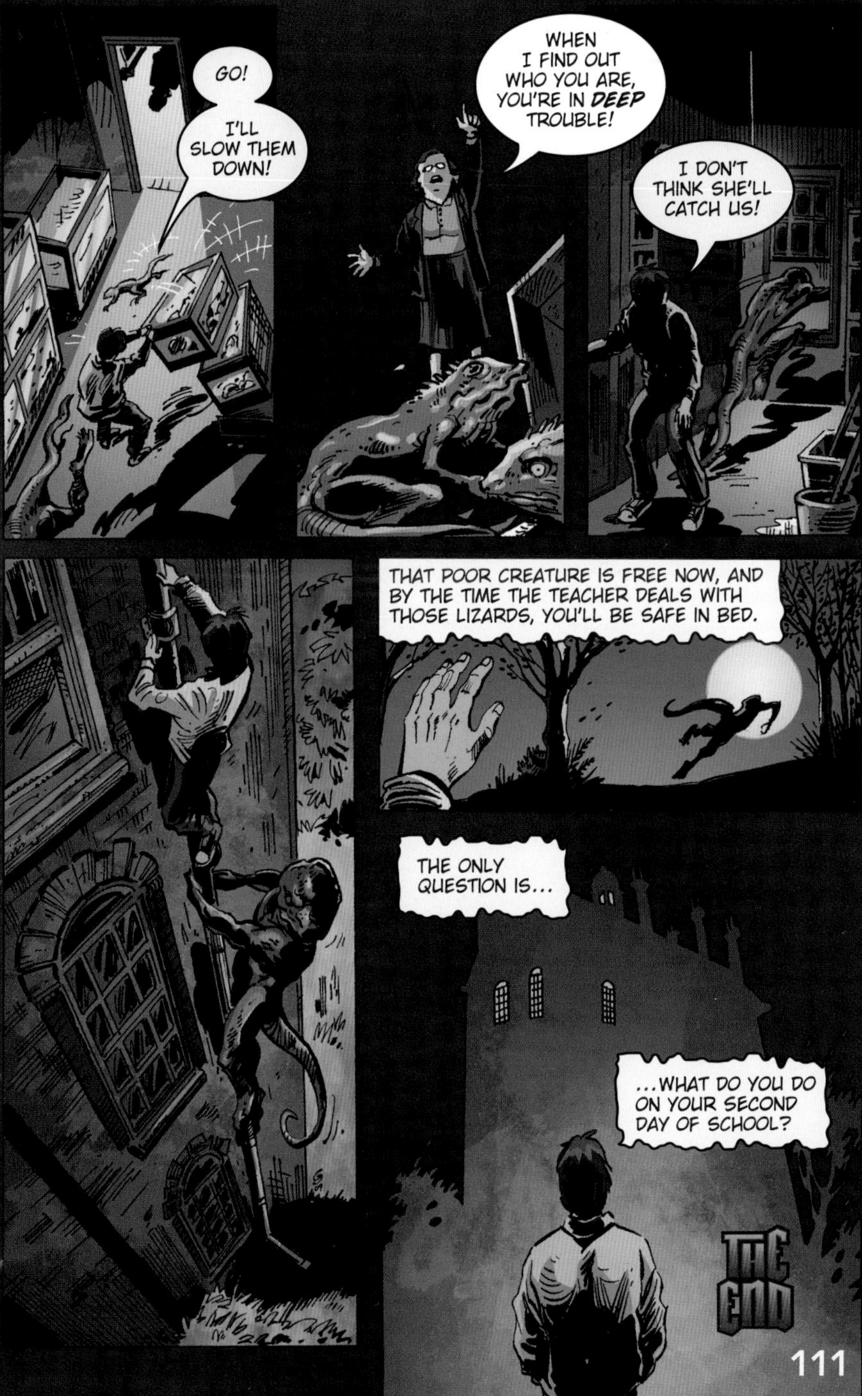
GO!
I'LL SLOW THEM DOWN!
WHEN I FIND OUT WHO YOU ARE, YOU'RE IN DEEP TROUBLE!
I DON'T THINK SHE'LL CATCH US!
THAT POOR CREATURE IS FREE NOW, AND BY THE TIME THE TEACHER DEALS WITH THOSE LIZARDS, YOU'LL BE SAFE IN BED.
THE ONLY QUESTION IS...
...WHAT DO YOU DO ON YOUR SECOND DAY OF SCHOOL?
THE END

WHICH TWISTED JOURNEYS® WILL YOU TRY NEXT?